A NECESSARY MARRIAGE

Enid Meredith is astonished when Richard Cummings, a friend and budding author, asks her to marry him. His reasons are financial, as he must marry quickly to fulfil the strange demands of his mother's will. Richard and Enid make a pact — friendship only and a quiet divorce at some future date. But as their lives become complicated, Enid's mental and emotional resources are stretched to breaking point. Will a solution come to light and enable them to start a new life afresh?

Books by Sylvia E. Kirk
in the Linford Romance Library:

A DOUBTING LOVE

SYLVIA E. KIRK

A NECESSARY MARRIAGE

Complete and Unabridged

LINFORD
Leicester

First published in Great Britain in 1994 by
Robert Hale Limited
London

First Linford Edition
published November 1995
by arrangement with
Robert Hale Limited
London

British Library CIP Data

Kirk, Sylvia E.
A necessary marriage.—Large print ed.—
Linford romance library
I. Title II. Series
823.914 [F]

ISBN 0–7089–7788–X

Published by
F. A. Thorpe (Publishing) Ltd.
Anstey, Leicestershire

Set by Words & Graphics Ltd.
Anstey, Leicestershire
Printed and bound in Great Britain by
T. J. Press (Padstow) Ltd., Padstow, Cornwall

This book is printed on acid-free paper

1

THE shop door swung shut behind Enid, and she stood immobile for a moment, too stunned and shaken to move. People began brushing past her, a small child blundered into her legs, and slowly she began to walk, turning instinctively in the direction of her flat. Her knees were shaking and she felt sick. It had been an ugly, shocking scene in the shop, made worse by the fact that it was totally unexpected. She had realised that Mrs Hatherley disliked her, but the sheer hatred glaring at her out of the woman's narrowed eyes had completely unnerved her, coming out of the blue as it had.

Enid paused again, took a steadying breath, then crossed the road, realising dimly that it had started to rain, that she didn't have an umbrella, and that unless she hurried she would be soaked before she reached home. She quickened her pace a little, trying to control her whirling thoughts, but the awful fact was coming home to her more clearly with every second that passed — Mrs Hatherley had sacked her, dismissed her on the spot — she was out of a job. Total disaster had overtaken her, what was she to do now?

Puddles were forming on the pavements and water began to run down the gutters, and she felt a small cold trickle starting down her neck, while limp hair plastered itself uncomfortably across her damp forehead. Her feet were wet too, and as she dragged herself miserably up the stone steps which led to her flat tears gathered in the corners of her eyes. She blinked them away, suddenly angry with herself — crying wouldn't help.

She fumbled in her handbag for her door key, searching the corners with her cold wet fingers, but it eluded her, and in a fit of sudden irritation she turned the bag upside down and shook it violently several times. The key fell out, and so did everything else — lipstick, powder compact, handkerchief, money, rolling perversely in every direction.

"Oh, damn!" she exclaimed, bending to retrieve them, then jumped as a voice behind her said:

"Hard luck! Here, let me help you."

She turned and saw Richard Cummings, who lived in the flat above hers, diving after a pound coin and finally trapping it by the skirting board.

"Thanks," she muttered as he handed it to her. "Stupid of me."

She thought he would make some suitable remark and walk away, but instead he stood there, looking intently at her.

"Are you all right?" he asked, and there was concern in his voice. "You look very pale."

"I — " she stopped, her voice refusing to obey her, then, before she could stop herself, blurted: "I've just been sacked."

"Oh, lord, I am sorry," Richard said. "I really am. What — what happened? Do you want to talk about it? Not that it's my business if you don't."

For a moment she stared at him, speechless, then the real sympathy in his gaze reached her, and she managed a brief, twisted smile.

"M'm," she nodded, and he said:

"Come on, the heat's on in my flat. I'll make us some tea, you look as if you could do with a cup."

She went up the stairs with him, leaving damp impressions on the worn carpet, and he pushed open the flat door and ushered her in, closing the door quietly behind them.

"Get that wet coat off, I'll put it in front of the radiator," he said, taking it from her. "Wait, I'll get you a towel for your hair."

He disappeared briefly, coming back with a large thick green towel, and she took it with a muttered word of thanks. Then he vanished again, reappearing with two steaming mugs and a plate of biscuits on a tray.

"I don't know if you take sugar or not," he said. "But I've put some in — good for shock."

Enid gave her hair one last rub, smiled her thanks, and took the proffered mug. Richard was watching her, still with concern in his brown eyes, and after a moment he said:

"Why were you sacked? I thought you were good at your job and quite an expert on antiques."

"I thought I was, too," Enid said ruefully. "It was so *stupid*, Richard — someone brought a vase in this morning and showed it to me. She thought it was valuable, and after I'd looked at it I was pretty sure it was a fake. Mr Hatherley wasn't there but Mrs Hatherley was, and she interrupted what I was saying and told this woman I didn't really know, it would be better to wait until Mr Hatherley got back. Well, I didn't mind that — two opinions are better than one, so the woman left the vase and I went out to lunch."

She stopped, and Richard said:

"Go on."

"When I got back from lunch there was the vase, smashed on the floor. It was in little pieces, Richard — I don't think anyone *could* have mended it even if it was worth it, which I don't think it was."

"Who broke it?" Richard asked.

"Well, I think it must have been Mrs Hatherley," Enid said, frowning. "Unless . . ."

"Unless what?" he asked.

"There's a cat there, but it doesn't usually come into the shop," Enid said. "It's either outside in the garden or upstairs in the Hatherleys' flat. It *could* have knocked the vase over but Mrs Hatherley had put it in a drawer, though I suppose she could have taken it out again to look at it."

"And left it in some precarious position," Richard nodded. "It's possible, I suppose, if she was interrupted. What

6

happened then?"

"Mrs Hatherley was in the back, so I called her. She came in, saw the pieces and accused me of breaking it deliberately because I'd made a mistake and didn't want Mr Hatherley to see the vase and expose my incompetence."

"Rubbish!" Richard exclaimed.

"That's what I said, unfortunately," Enid gave a wry smile. "Then she really flew into a temper — called me all sorts of names, and finally said I was sacked and to get out. Instant dismissal, in fact."

Her lips trembled suddenly, and Richard gave her shoulder a comforting squeeze.

"She sounds an absolute bitch," he said frankly. "But what about Mr Hatherley? Surely he'll have something to say about this."

"Well, he might," Enid shrugged. "But what can he do? It's really my word against his wife's, and she's a very forceful sort of woman. I've had a feeling for some time that she didn't

7

like me, she was just tolerating me because I was useful and because Dad used to work for Mr Hatherley before — before he died, and they were very good friends. But I do wish I knew what I'd done to make her hate me, because she does, Richard."

Richard looked at her, smiling a little. Her damp hair was turning into little, shining brown curls clustering round her ears, her large deep blue eyes were looking up into his, a puzzled expression in them, her small shapely hands were clasped round the mug, and two rounded knees protruded from under her skirt.

"Don't you know?" he said drily, and suddenly, she flushed.

"Oh no, Richard, honestly! You don't think Mr Hatherley — of course he hasn't — we haven't — "

"I don't think anything of the sort," Richard said. "But she might, Enid. You're a very attractive girl, she might simply be jealous."

"Well, she's stupid, then," Enid said

flatly. "And quite wrong."

There was a pause, while Enid stared broodingly into space, then Richard cut briskly into her reverie.

"Did she give you any money?" he asked. "She should have done."

"My salary till the end of the month, you mean?" Enid shook her head. "She said something about my not being entitled because of the vase, which she and Mr Hatherley would have to pay for. They will, of course."

"H'm." Richard frowned thoughtfully. "Bit of a mess, isn't it?"

"Yes, it is. I — I do really need the job, Richard."

"Who doesn't?" His smile was almost as strained as hers. "You'll get another one, Enid, don't worry about that."

"I hope so. Another of the things she yelled at me was that she would see I didn't get a reference."

"Charming." Richard scowled. "There's such a thing as wrongful dismissal, Enid."

"I know that, but I can't prove I

didn't break the vase."

"And she can't prove you *did*," he pointed out. "Want some more tea?"

"Oh, yes please," she said gratefully, and she stretched out her legs as he vanished once more into the kitchen.

She looked round the room, feeling curious. In size it was an exact replica of her own small lounge downstairs, but there the resemblance ended. The whole of two walls were covered in book shelves, and the shelves were stacked high with books and folders of every description. There was a word processor standing on a heavy table in one corner, two shabby armchairs on either side of the fireplace, and four ordinary chairs arranged round the room. The carpet was faded and a little worn in places, and the curtains had definitely seen better days. She knew that Richard was a writer, and now she wondered if he was hard up, too . . .

He came back and handed her the

10

refilled mug, and as she smiled her thanks she studied him surreptitiously over the rim of it.

He was a tall, rather thin man with thick unruly auburn hair, casually dressed in a sweater and trousers which like his carpet had seen better days. He wasn't handsome but he had deep brown eyes and a mobile mouth which she knew broke very easily into an engaging grin.

"That's enough talk about me," she said impulsively. "How are you getting on? How's the writing going?"

"Not too bad." He wrinkled his nose thoughtfully. "My first novel comes out next month."

"Richard, that's marvellous!" she exclaimed. "Terrific! I hope it'll be a great success."

"So do I, or I've quarrelled — I mean I've wasted nearly a year on it for nothing," he said, rather grimly, and silence fell.

Who had he quarrelled with, Enid wondered, and why? Just as she was trying to think of some tactful way to ask him, he said suddenly:

"It was my father I quarrelled with, Enid, there's no real reason why you shouldn't know. He wanted me to join the family business and I wouldn't."

"Well," Enid ventured slowly. "If you didn't want to then there was no real point, was there? You wouldn't have been happy and you probably wouldn't have been very efficient."

"Try telling that to my dear old Dad," Richard said, and there was a bitter edge to his voice. "He practically threw me out of the house."

"I'm sorry," Enid said with quiet sincerity. "That must have been awful for you. I don't think my father would ever have done that."

"What was he like? Your father, I mean," Richard asked unexpectedly.

"Nice. Very cultured, very artistic and hopeless about money," Enid said, truthfully. Then, before she could stop herself, she went on: "Which is why I need a job badly, Richard — he left debts, you see, and I'm still paying them off."

"That's bad luck," Richard frowned. "I had no idea. Do you owe much?"

"About two thousand. Not much by today's standards, but when it's got to come out of your salary every month . . . "

"Yes, I can see why you need that job." Richard's frown deepened. "Enid, I'm not really qualified to advise you, I think you need a solicitor, or perhaps — perhaps you should try to talk to Mr Hatherley."

"M'm," Enid nodded. "You may be right — I'll go round in the morning and see him."

"Good." Richard nodded. "Mrs Hatherley might have cooled down by then."

"I certainly hope so," Enid said, and remembered the woman's spiteful, furious face — was it possible that she really believed Enid had broken the vase for the ridiculous reason she'd given?

"That's enough about me," Enid said. "How are you, Richard, and how is — what's her name — Gina?"

"I'm fine, and so is she," he replied. "We're getting married soon."

"Oh, that's great!" Enid exclaimed. "Congratulations."

"Thanks," Richard's grin flashed out. "You OK now?"

"Yes, thanks, and thanks for the shoulder. Richard, I must go now, I've taken up enough of your time already."

"A pleasure."

He gave her a quick hug and she left, feeling marginally more hopeful, and as she walked into the familiar little flat her spirits rose again. Surely Mr Hatherley would make his wife see how stupid she was being! Enid eyed the phone thoughtfully — was it worth while phoning the shop and asking to speak to him now? She paused, thinking it over, then reluctantly decided against it. It was too soon, even Mrs Hatherley might think better of things if she had a chance to reflect a little.

Meanwhile, what to do? It seemed too soon to start looking at the 'situations vacant' page in the local paper, so perhaps a quiet evening with an interesting book might be a good solution. Outside the rain was still coming down with undiminished enthusiasm, the wind had risen, and as she pulled the curtains to hide the dismal scene Enid pulled a face. It was an awful afternoon.

She went into the small kitchen and looked in the fridge. Something quick, simple and delicious, she decided, then straightened up as firm light footsteps went past her front door and died away as they went down the outside steps. Richard, on his way to meet his beautiful fiancée, Georgina Wood. Enid didn't know her very well, they had only met twice, once in a pub and once on the stairs, but she was lovely — a cool, flaxen fair blonde with a sweet, slightly husky voice. If her nature matched her looks then Richard was lucky, Enid thought, and why shouldn't he be? He was a thoroughly nice person.

Enid's mind went suddenly to what he had said about his father. It was a pity they had quarrelled but she couldn't blame Richard for sticking to his guns. Trying to make anyone do what they didn't want to was stupid — what was that American expression? 'A hiding to nothing?' Still, if Richard's book was a success then maybe his father would see sense.

For the rest of the evening Enid tried to put the affair of the vase out of her mind, but it kept coming back to haunt her. Someone must have taken it out of the drawer, and that could only have been Mrs Hatherley, so why hadn't she put it back or at least stood it in a safe position? Unless, of course, as Richard suggested she had been called to the phone, or someone had come into the shop and she had simply forgotten it. It could have been Willow the cat, of course, but he very seldom came into the shop. But cats were unpredictable, he could have knocked the vase down and strolled off, nonchalantly waving an unconcerned brown tail . . .

It was impossible to be sure, and impatiently Enid went to the television and turned it on. Anything to occupy her mind until she had really decided what to do . . .

When the knock sounded on her door she jumped, then got up slowly, wondering who it was. She looked through the spy hole all the flat owners had, and saw Mr Hatherley standing there, shaking water from his big black umbrella. She opened the door, standing aside for him to come in, and he walked past her into the flat. She closed the door and turned to face him, her face pale and grave. They eyed each other for a few seconds, then he smiled briefly.

"Hello, Enid," he said quietly. "I hope I'm not disturbing you."

"No, not at all," she replied, switching the television off. "Please, sit down."

He perched himself on the edge of an armchair, obviously very ill at ease. Twice he started to speak, then stopped, and she decided to take the initiative.

"If you've come about that vase," she said bluntly, "I didn't break it, it was in bits when I came back from lunch."

"H'm," he nodded rather wearily. "Yes, I accept that, but unfortunately Polly insists that you did. She says she left the vase in a drawer so it had to be you, Enid. I really am sorry but she sticks to her story and as there weren't any witnesses . . . "

His voice trailed off, and Enid, indignation surging through her, demanded:

"Well, tell me this, then — why did I do it? What was the point?"

Mr Hatherley didn't reply directly to that, instead he said quietly:

"I could overrule her, Enid, give you your job back and say let's forget it, but it would be uncomfortable for you and Polly — "

" — would give you hell," Enid

interrupted, and he gave a wry, half embarrassed little smile.

"What I suggest is this," he said. "I've thought about it, Enid. I'll give you proper redundancy pay and a good reference, you should be able to get a job quite quickly with your qualifications. Nobody need know anything about the vase, which I think was a fake, too."

"Did you have to pay much for it?" Enid asked, and he gave a rueful smile.

"More than it was worth, but I had to keep the owner quiet. I couldn't have her going around saying we'd smashed a valuable vase and refused to give her the proper price."

"It's been an expensive day for you, hasn't it?" Suddenly, Enid was sorry for him. "I am sorry."

"So am I," Mr Hatherley rose slowly to his feet, "I'll send you that reference, and here — " he held out an envelope — "take this. And Enid — don't mention that damned vase to anyone else, will you? If there's anything else I can do let me know."

"Thank you." Forcing down her feelings, she accepted the envelope, then belatedly remembered her manners. "You wouldn't like a cup of coffee, would you? I'm sorry, I put that badly — I mean, I haven't got anything stronger."

"No, thanks." He smiled, and moved to the door. "Goodbye, Enid, and good luck."

"Goodbye." She watched him go, muttering under her breath: "Good luck to you, too — married to Polly you'll need it."

Richard had been right, Enid thought, as she slowly returned to her chair. Mrs Hatherley had been jealous of her, totally without cause — poor Mr Hatherley, what a life she would lead him if he didn't stand up to her, but perhaps standing up to people wasn't Mr Hatherley's strong suit. He tended to give in if the pressure was strong enough . . .

She opened the envelope and took out the cheque. Mr Hatherley had given her three months' salary, which would help to clear her debt to the bank, but what about another job?

'I'll have to start looking tomorrow,' she thought, and it wasn't a pleasant thought.

She had worked for Mr Hatherley since she had left college, and there simply wasn't another antique shop in the town that she could remember, even given they wanted an assistant. But a job of some kind she must have, so in the morning she must pay the Job Centre a visit.

★ ★ ★

It was a totally new experience for Enid to join a queue of people, mostly young, some of them obviously dispirited, and state her qualifications to the severe looking young woman on the other side of the table. Fortunately the severe look was deceptive, and Enid received

21

sympathetic treatment but very little hope of a job.

"You see, Miss Meredith, you're really over qualified for anything we have to offer here at the moment," the girl said, looking worried. "There are one or two shop assistant's jobs, but one is in a dress shop and the other is in a bakery."

"Not really me," Enid dredged up a smile. "Thanks, anyway."

"You'll let us know if you find something, won't you?" The girl said, after Enid had signed the unfamiliar form. "And come in at the right times, won't you?"

Enid nodded and got up, yielding her place to a morose looking young man with an ear-ring in his ear and tattered jeans. Feeling completely depressed, she went slowly into the street. What now? Should she tell her bank manager what had happened and ask his advice about the debt, or wait a week or so in the apparently faint hope that a suitable job might present itself?

She banked Mr Hatherley's cheque, then went for an aimless stroll through the town, working out her finances in her head as she went. She could manage for a month or two, maybe even longer, and then . . .

Finally she returned home, and as she turned the key in the lock she heard footsteps coming down the stairs which led to Richard's flat, and looked up. It was Richard, and she started to speak, then the greeting died on her lips and she stood, staring at him.

His face was pale, there were black marks under his eyes as if he hadn't slept, and he looked dazed, as if he had suffered some severe shock.

"*Richard?*" she queried, and he gave her the ghost of a smile.

"Hello, Enid," he said, and even his voice was strange, flat and defeated.

"Are you all right?" she blurted, knowing that it was a silly question because obviously he wasn't.

He looked back at her in silence for a moment, then shook his head.

23

"No, I'm not." He hesitated, then said: "You may as well know. Gina broke off our engagement last night."

"Oh *no*," Enid exclaimed, aghast. "Oh, Richard, I'm so sorry."

"So 'm I." He ran his hand wearily through his hair. "It appears there's another guy, somebody called Jo Marsh — she's known him for some time, apparently."

"Then why didn't she tell you before?" Enid asked, indignantly, and Richard shrugged.

"God knows. I didn't know a damned thing about it, Enid, I had no idea."

"Come in and have some coffee," she suggested, and he walked slowly past her, moving with the uncertain gait of someone in shock.

Resisting the temptation of steering him into a chair, she went into the kitchen, wishing she had some whisky because if ever anyone needed a stiff drink it was Richard. But she had cut down on all unnecessary things, so a strong coffee, well sugared, would have to do.

He took it with a murmur of thanks, and she sat down opposite him, searching for something clever and comforting to say to him, but nothing came. What *could* she say without sounding trite and stupid? 'These things happen.' 'You're better off without a girl like that, there'll be someone else.'

She waited, wondering if he wanted to talk about it and preparing herself to listen, but instead he asked her what her own position was, and she gave him a brief resumé of the situation.

"Not very hopeful, eh?" he commented. "What will you do?"

"Well, if I can't find anything to do with antiques, I'll have to try something different," she said. "It's all I can do."

He put down his coffee mug and looked thoughtfully at her, and she looked back, smiling slightly. His next remark really surprised her.

"Do you have a boy friend, Enid? Sorry if that's personal, but do you?"

"Well, no, not at the moment," she said. "Why?"

There was a pause while he seemed to gather his thoughts, then he said slowly:

"If I tell you something, will you listen?"

"Yes, of course I'll listen." Intrigued, she settled back in her chair, while Richard looked round the room as if for inspiration. "Right."

"My mother," he began slowly, as if picking his words. "Left rather a peculiar will."

"Oh?" Enid said enquiringly, and he nodded.

"Very peculiar," he said. "Quite dotty, in fact. A third of her money to Dad, a third to my sister, and a third to me, on condition I was married by the time I was twenty-eight."

"Why twenty-eight?" Enid asked blankly, and Richard smiled briefly.

"Because that's the age Dad was when they were married and she thought it was the right time. Silly, isn't it?"

"It does seem odd," Enid commented. "So what happens if you're *not* married by that time?"

"Then I don't get it, it goes to Dad," Richard said flatly. "Enid, I shall be twenty-eight in two months time."

"What are you going to do?" Enid's mouth fell open in dismay. "Contest the will?"

"I think it's too late for that, and I might not win, anyway. Besides, I thought Gina and I were going to be married, there was no point doing it before. I really need that money, I've earned next to nothing with the writing so far. I'm paying the rent with the money I've earned from part time jobs, and I'm almost broke."

"I had no idea," Enid said. "Richard, I really am sorry."

There was another long pause, then he drew a deep, ragged breath, sat bolt upright in his chair, and said:

"Enid, will you do it? Will you marry me?"

2

FOR a stunned moment Enid thought she had misheard him, or misunderstood, then she saw his expression and realised that she hadn't. Richard had asked her to marry him, and was sitting there waiting tensely for an answer. She swallowed, searching desperately in her mind for something to say, but nothing came, and Richard gave a sudden, almost apologetic smile.

"Enid, I — I'm sorry," he said. "I shouldn't have sprung it on you like that, only I'm desperate. Listen, this is what I thought. We get married as soon as possible — Registry Office, I think — and we live together for a year or so, perhaps a bit longer, long enough to make it look authentic, and then we part, quietly and with no hard feelings. I'll give you — well, I'll make it worth your while. It would get both of us off the hook financially."

He stopped, Enid took a deep breath, then asked:

"Do we — do we sleep together?"

"Not if you don't want to," he said. "But we must make it look authentic, not a — a put up job, that's essential or it won't work."

"It's very — very unethical," Enid commented, in a flat expressionless voice totally unlike her own, and Richard nodded.

"Yes, I know it is, but Mum really meant me to have that money, she thought Gina and I were permanent, and I can't blame her for that, so did I. I never thought Gina would do this to me." Suddenly, he looked like a hurt child. "So it was a double shock when it happened. We're friends, aren't we, and we're both sick of being hard up? I'll get you off the hook with your bank straight away, I promise you that."

Enid ran her hand through her hair and sighed.

In a way Richard was right, morally that money should come to him, so who would they be defrauding? No one, really . . .

"Have — have your father and your sister got their share?" she asked, and Richard nodded.

"Yes, and luckily Penny was already married or God knows what conditions Mum might have dreamed up for her," he smiled normally for the first time, and Enid smiled too. "Fortunately Mum liked her husband."

"I see." Enid got up and walked over to the window, staring unseeingly out at the drizzling rain. "If — if I agree, where will we live? Your flat or mine?"

"Yours, I guess." Richard joined her at the window. "It is yours, isn't it? I mean, you don't have a mortgage."

"No." Enid shook her head. "Dad did listen to me for once over that."

"Parents," Richard said in tones of resigned exasperation, and Enid nodded agreement.

"And if — or when we decide to

part, what happens then?" she asked.

"I leave, not you, and you get some of the money. I suppose legally you might be entitled to half, we'd have to discuss it."

"Yes, I see." She bit her lip, thinking ruefully that this wasn't the sort of marriage she had dreamed of . . . but Richard was a friend, she had known him for over a year, and he was a nice guy, and why shouldn't he have that money? And it would be nice to be solvent again, perhaps with some money of her own she could do what she liked with.

"All right, Richard," she heard herself say. "I agree, I'll do it."

"Great," he breathed, and his arm came round her in a fierce, hard hug. "Thanks, Enid. I promise you won't be sorry."

She stood for a moment in the circle of his arm, a prey to so many conflicting emotions she couldn't speak, then she released herself gently and went back to her chair.

"We've got a lot to talk about," she said as Richard re-seated himself opposite her. "May I just ask you — do you know precisely how much money you're actually getting?"

"Yes," Richard nodded. "It's a hundred and fifty thousand, Enid."

"Oh. I didn't think it would be as much as that."

"You see why I didn't want to pass it up," he said. "Or let Dad have it, he's got quite enough already. Enid, would you like to go out to lunch, somewhere quiet where we can talk?"

"Yes, I do feel a bit — hollow," Enid agreed, and he laughed.

"I'm not surprised, it's nearly two o'clock. Enid, I can't tell you how relieved I am, bless you."

She smiled and went into her bedroom for her coat, her knees trembling a little. As she slipped into the coat she caught sight of her face in the mirror, very pale, blue eyes bigger than ever, and she drew another deep, steadying breath. It had been a

33

traumatic few days, and it wasn't over yet . . .

"I'm sorry, we'll have to walk," Richard said, as they went downstairs together. "My old heap is in the garage being put together again. That's one of the things I'm going to do, Enid — get a decent car. You haven't got one, have you?"

"No," she shook her head. "I couldn't afford it in my present hard up state. Where shall we go?"

"That little place next to the jewellers," Richard said, sliding his hand under her arm. "It's quiet. We'll get a corner table if we can."

She fell into step with him, thinking how much things had changed. Nothing was the same, because now there was Richard and somehow they would both have to appear to be a loving, happily married couple with all that entailed. For one thing, they would have to share a bedroom. It was a startling but not altogether unpleasant thought, and she pointed this out to Richard as soon as they had settled themselves at the luckily vacant corner table.

"You're right," he said. "How about twin beds?"

"M'm, OK. Why don't we have a double one, if anyone asks?"

"I've got a dodgy back," he replied promptly. "Actually, I have, I got it playing rugby. It's not that bad but we can always make out it's worse than it is."

Enid nodded, and Richard fished a small notebook out of his pocket, saying:

"Maybe we should make a note of what we've got to do, Enid — there isn't all that much time."

The waitress appeared for their order, and they began to list the things that must be done. It was Enid who suggested that Richard move in with her straight away to save paying unnecessary rent.

"I'd like to," he said. "There won't be any furniture to shift, just my clothes, books and the word processor. I've got to have that, Enid."

"Yes, I know. Listen, why don't we put your stuff in the small bedroom? Then you can write in peace."

"Good idea." Richard made a quick note. "Enid, your bed, that will have to go, won't it?"

"Yes. Maybe the furniture people will take it in part exchange for the twin beds."

Richard looked thoughtfully at her, smiling a little.

"You know, Enid, for a girl who looks — I don't know, so *decorative*, you're a surprisingly good organiser."

"Thanks for the decorative," she smiled at him. "I learned to organise, Richard, I had Dad to watch out for — he was hopeless at anything like that."

"I liked him, though," Richard said thoughtfully. "He knew such a lot about art and music, and he seemed so *kind*."

"He was," Enid said huskily. "He

36

just thought that if he ignored bills they would walk away and pay themselves."

"Would that were true," Richard said sadly. "What's the first job when we leave here, Enid?"

"The Registry Office?" she suggested. "Then the furniture shop to look at some twin beds."

"Right," Richard nodded, then a dismayed expression crossed his face. "Enid, I haven't got much money, how about you?"

They added up their joint resources, and discovered that they could afford the licence fee and the twin beds. Richard heaved a sigh of relief.

"Thank God for that," he said. "I haven't got a thing I can sell except my camera."

"I haven't got a thing to sell period," Enid said ruefully, and his hand came over and covered hers.

"I noticed," he said gently. "That's where all your pretty china went, wasn't it? Settling bills."

"M'm." She swallowed hard, forcing

37

back unexpected tears. "Shall we have some coffee?"

Richard opted for the coffee, and the rest of the afternoon was spent working their way methodically through the various tasks they had set themselves. Fortunately the rain had stopped, and as they went back upstairs Richard said:

"Thank heaven that's done. I must write to Mum's solicitors and tell them the good news. Enid, I've just thought of something — we should have a wedding reception, it would look odd if we didn't."

Enid paused, key in hand, startled. Somehow she hadn't thought as far ahead as a wedding reception, but Richard was right, they must do something. She opened the door and they went inside.

"Who would *you* invite?" she asked, and Richard gnawed his lip, frowning.

"Penny would come, and her husband if he could get away," he said slowly. "How about you?"

"I've got one or two friends," she said, wriggling out of her coat, while Richard automatically helped. "Richard, what — what about your father?"

"No thank you," Richard said, his mouth suddenly hard. "He's the last person I want, and he wouldn't come, anyway."

Enid's lips parted, but she said nothing. Evidently Richard's disagreement with his father had gone deep . . . there seemed no point in discussing it, so she said:

"How about someone from your mother's solicitors, then? To prove that you *have* got married."

"Brilliant!" he exclaimed. "Yes, of course, you're right . . . anyone else?"

"I'd have liked Mr Hatherley," she said slowly. "He and Dad were such good friends."

"Well, ask him then, and that virago of a woman of his," Richard said, grinning. "They can only say 'no'."

"M'm. Richard, I've just thought

39

of something else — shouldn't you let your landlord know you're moving out?"

"Yes. I'll write to him and the solicitors tonight."

"Would you like some tea, Richard?" she asked, and he nodded.

In the kitchen she took one of the long deep breaths she seemed to need lately, and found that Richard had followed her in.

"I thought it might be a good idea if you showed me where you keep everything," he said, half apologetically. "Or would you rather not?"

She opened all the cupboards, showed him the contents of the fridge freezer, and explained how to use the washing machine.

"You're a lot tidier than me," he commented, as she made the tea. "Enid, *when* did those furniture people say they were delivering?"

"Tomorrow afternoon, I'll have to stay in," she said. "Could you bring the biscuit tin?"

"Would it be all right if I moved in with you after they've gone?" he asked, and she nodded.

"Why not?" she said quietly. "I'll help you get your stuff down if you like."

"Thanks," he said. "You're a great girl, Enid."

She laughed, and he smiled, then the smile went and instinctively she knew he was thinking of Gina.

Once more she could think of nothing to say to comfort him, but she slid her hand over his for a brief moment before she poured their tea, and his smile came back momentarily.

"If — if you want to talk about — about Gina, I don't mind," she said quietly. "If it makes you feel better."

"What can I say?" He took the steaming mug. "I loved the girl, I thought she felt the same way. She didn't."

"M'm. Well, there's one thing, I suppose, Richard — she isn't a gold digger or she'd have stuck to you for the money."

"Suppose you're right there. Unless, of course — " his expression became cynical, almost bitter — "she thought this Jo Marsh guy is a better proposition than a struggling would-be writer."

"Did she — did she tell you anything about him?"

"Not a lot." He looked down at his hands, frowning. "He's something in the City — could be anything for all I know."

There seemed nothing more to be said, and Enid levered the lid off the biscuit tin in silence. Richard took one absently, Enid followed suit, and when Richard spoke again it was about something different.

"Invitation cards!" he exclaimed. "To the wedding, should we use them?"

"Of course." Annoyed with herself for not having thought of that, Enid made a note on their list. "I'll see to it. How many?"

"Ten should more than cover it." He said. "This isn't any girl's idea of a wedding, is it, Enid? I am sorry."

"Don't be." She smiled reassuringly at him. "I don't like big weddings anyway, whatever the circumstances."

"A dress!" he exclaimed. "You must have a new dress!"

"That's all right," she said reassuringly. "I've got one in the wardrobe I've never worn, and shoes and a hat to go with it. What about you, do you have a decent suit?"

"Yes, luckily." He nodded. "I can just about afford a new shirt."

"Buttonholes!" Enid said suddenly. "I'll order them."

"Can you think of anything else?" Richard asked, then an almost embarrassed expression flitted across his face. "Er — Enid, what — what about a honeymoon?"

"Oh," she said, a little blankly. "Um . . ."

"What do we do?" he asked. "I don't know exactly when I'll get the money, and we can't afford to go away without it, can we?"

"I know. We're waiting for better weather and you're very busy planning another novel," Enid said. "We're probably going in about two months time. How's that?"

"Best we can do, I suppose." He nodded. "So long as we both tell the same story if anyone asks us."

"Yes," she nodded in her turn. "Richard, your books — we'd better get some book shelves, hadn't we?"

"I never thought of that. Yes, we had . . . Enid, I'd better go and see to those letters. Can you think of anything else we should do?"

"Not at the moment." She shook her head. "If I do, I'll make a note of it."

He stood up, looking down at her for a moment, then bent and kissed her cheek.

"Thanks, Enid," he said huskily. "See you in the morning."

He was gone, and she closed the

44

door behind him, filled with a sudden sense of total unreality. What was she *doing*? What were they both doing? For a brief few seconds she almost ran upstairs after him to tell him she couldn't go through with it, then she remembered her promise to him and stopped.

Sinking down in an armchair she sat with her head in her hands, thinking. This marriage wasn't what either of them would have wanted, but then neither of them had really envisaged the situations in which they found themselves. Richard, cast off by his father, rejected by his fiancée at the eleventh hour, herself jobless and in debt through no fault of her own — why shouldn't they try to retrieve the situation? And if they were deceiving other people at least they were being honest with each other . . .

Forcing herself to be practical she looked at their list again, added one or two things, then put it away and tidied the flat. Tomorrow the whole place would be different, Richard's things would be *ensconced* in the second bedroom, the twin beds would arrive . . . sheets and blankets! Did she have enough?

Diving into the linen cupboard she decided that she had, but matching duvets would have to be bought some time, and they joined the other items on the list.

Then, exhaustion sweeping unexpectedly over her, she opened a handy tin of soup and drank it slowly, wondering wearily how Richard was getting on upstairs. Had he written his letters? And how was he feeling? Reaction might have set in, and she wondered if she should go up and see if he was all right. Then she decided against it — recovering from the shock of Gina's rejection was a private thing in a way, there seemed very little she, Enid, could do about it . . .

Her mind went to Richard's father. Why had he been so against his son being a writer? Disappointment she

46

could understand, anger too, but total rejection? It seemed so extreme . . . but there *were* men like that, and women, too . . .

"Parents," she muttered, and grinned ruefully, remembering the bills she hadn't realised her father was running up.

But if her father hadn't had any money sense he had been unfailingly kind and gentle, and it was he who had passed on his love of beautiful things to her. She could remember him showing her an old silver teapot when she was about five, showing her the fine engraving on it and explaining how he knew it was genuinely so old. She had stroked it with a stubby baby finger, and he had stroked her leaf brown hair away from her eyes, smiling lovingly at her . . . she missed him cruelly.

Then, so tired that she could hardly keep her eyes open, she got ready for bed and fell asleep almost as soon as her head touched the pillow.

She was awakened the next morning

by someone ringing her doorbell, and struggling into a negligee she went to open it. Richard was standing there, fully dressed, and she blinked at him, smothering a yawn.

"You're up early," she said. "Come in."

"It's nine o'clock," he protested with a half smile. "Did you oversleep?"

"I must have done," she said. "Want some tea?"

"Let me make it," he suggested. "While you get dressed. Would you like toast as well?"

"M'm, thanks." Stifling another yawn she hurried into the bathroom, hoping that Richard wouldn't let the kettle boil dry or cinder the toast, and thinking that he might as well get familiar with her kitchen appliances as he would be living with her for the foreseeable future.

Cold water splashed in her face woke her up, and a few minutes later she was sitting opposite Richard, munching toast and discussing plans.

"I thought we could bring some of the stuff down this morning," Richard suggested. "There'll be a lot to do this afternoon. I wrote those letters, by the way."

"Good." She glanced across the table at him. He looked pale and heavy eyed, but calm. "Are you OK?"

"M'm." He nodded, his eyes searching her face. "Are you? You haven't changed your mind?"

"No. Have you?"

"No."

"Good. We'll get started on your things after breakfast, if you like."

They toiled up and down the stairs, carrying piles of books and folders, then Richard's word processor, his clothes and the contents of his fridge and cupboards.

"I'm worn out," he said, as the last packet and tin went tidily into Enid's food cupboard. "And so must you be — shall I shoot out and get us some fish and chips?"

"If you can afford it," she said,

49

getting down from the chair she'd been standing on. "Is there anything else?"

"I don't think so," he shook his head. "I'll go up for a last look after lunch. Right, I'm off, then. Shan't be long."

Enid went slowly to a chair and sat down with a grimace, easing off her shoes. Her legs were aching from climbing stairs, and her arms and shoulders felt stiff with the weight she had carried — Richard certainly had a lot of books, and they were all stacked round the walls in the second bedroom, while his word processor sat on the bed, looking curiously out of place. They would have to get a table for that . . .

After a few minutes she dragged herself out of the chair and set the table, feeling hungry, and hoping that Richard wouldn't be long. In a curious way she was getting used to having him around — he was good company, and again she wondered about Gina.

But nobody could define attraction of any kind, mental or physical, and Gina must have seen something in Jo Marsh that Richard didn't have. She felt curious about Gina — what did she do, what was her job? Where did she live? Richard hadn't told her and she hadn't asked him. Perhaps she *should* ask him, in case someone brought up the subject.

He returned a few minutes later with their lunch and as she slid the food on to plates she asked him to tell her a little about Gina. There was a momentary pause, then he said:

"She's twenty-four, she's a nurse, she works at St James Hospital."

"A *nurse*?" Enid stared at him, astonished, and he gave his now familiar sideways grin.

"Yes, it is surprising isn't it? Most people think she's a model or an actress, something like that."

"Where does she live?"

"She's got a flat near the hospital," he said, following her into the lounge.

"Quite a decent place, her father left her some money when he died."

"I wish mine had," Enid said feelingly. "Is her mother still around?"

"Yes, and she's got a brother in Australia."

"I see. Thanks, Richard, it wasn't just idle curiosity — I thought maybe I should know."

"Yes," he nodded, sliding the salt in her direction.

"Richard, you said your father was — well, reasonably well off, but I haven't a clue what *he* does, either."

"Haven't you really? Didn't I tell you? He's Cummings Constructions."

"The building people?" Enid stopped spearing a chip and stared at him again. "But they're — "

"Big. Yes, very, and Dad's the Big Boss." He made it sound like a particularly unpleasant disease. "And didn't I just know it."

"I see." Enid was silent for a moment, digesting this information. "Well, I can see why you said he didn't need any more money."

"M'm. Have you seen that enormous house just out of town on the Belford Road? That's his."

"Wow. The one you can just see through the trees from the top of a bus?"

"Yup." Richard dolloped tomato sauce on his fish with a grim smile. "'Abandon hope, all those who enter in'"

"It must have taken real — real guts to do what you did," Enid said slowly. "Richard, who did Penny marry?"

"A right hand man of Dad's, David Randall. He's OK. I tried to tell Dad he and Penny were the logical successors to him — Penny's a superb accountant, for instance, but he wouldn't hear of it. I was his only son and that was that, whether I liked it or not. Incidentally, I'm using a pseudonym for the novels, Enid — one of the things he yelled at me before I finally left was if I wanted to make a total fool of myself not to do it under his name."

"Charming," Enid muttered. "I really am sorry, Richard."

"So was I but it couldn't be helped." He smiled briefly. "Is there anything else you think you should know?"

"I can't think of anything at the moment." Enid thought it would take some time for her to digest what he had just said.

"While we're talking there is something we haven't discussed," he said suddenly. "And that's how much you get when we split. Or if," he added, with a sudden engaging smile.

"I hadn't thought about that," she said blankly. "But I *don't* want half, Richard, that's far too much."

"All right. How about thirty thousand, and I'll put you right with the bank?"

"That seems a lot, too," she ventured, but he shook his head.

"Not really when you consider I wouldn't be getting a penny without your help," he said. "Listen, Enid. With that you can move if you want, get a house, invest it, marry again . . . and

I'll have enough to buy my own flat and have something invested as well. I'm not fool enough to expect to get a bestseller right away, it rarely happens like that. Would you like a legal agreement?"

"No. No, I'd rather trust you. If someone finds out we've done that they might suspect we've conned your mother's solicitors."

"Serve them damned well right if we did," Richard said with a wicked grin. "They should have stopped her doing such a stupid thing. OK, Enid, that's settled, then. Shall I make some tea? Those delivery men could be here any minute."

★ ★ ★

It was a hectic afternoon. The twin beds came and were installed, Enid's old bed went out, together with the one from the second bedroom, and Richard stood in what was to be his study and ruefully surveyed the mess.

"We do need those shelves, Enid," he said, and they went out to see what they could find.

This took far longer than Enid thought it would, but eventually they settled on something, to be delivered within a few days, and they walked home, holding hands companionably.

"It's all coming together," Richard said, as they went into the flat. "It's going to be OK, Enid."

"I think so," she agreed, but even as she said it an odd feeling of unease passed over her, and she gave a quick, suppressed little shiver . . .

3

"WAKE up." Someone was shaking her, and Enid rolled over and peered blearily up at Richard, who was standing by the side of her bed with a mug in his hand. "It's half past eight."

"Oooh," Enid moaned, sitting up. Then she squinted at him and realised that he was fully dressed. "You're up."

"Yes, and I've had a shower and I've set the table for breakfast," he said smugly. "I take it from the way you became unconscious last night I didn't snore."

"Well, if you did I didn't hear you." She took the mug with a smile. "Thanks, Richard. Was your new bed comfortable?"

"Great," he said, perching himself on the end of hers. "How are you feeling?

My legs were killing me last night, I guess it was all that tramping about."

"All those stairs," she agreed. "What are we doing today?"

"Making sure all the loose ends are tied up, I suppose," he said seriously. "I'll have to let my publishers know my new address, and maybe I should let Penny know as well."

"You're still in touch with her, then?"

"Yes, she's a good kid." His tone was unexpectedly tender, and Enid thought that whatever his father had done it hadn't affected his affection for his sister.

"I hope Penny and David can come to the wedding," Enid said aloud. "Those invitation cards should be ready today, I'll collect them from the shop and we can get them posted."

"Right." He levered himself off the bed. "Now then, lazybones, get yourself cleaned up and we'll have breakfast."

He grinned and went, and Enid went slowly into the bathroom. As she stood under the shower it occurred to her that Richard was displaying commendable tact. He had waited for her to get undressed before coming to bed the night before, tapping the door, and he was obviously not going to hang around while she got dressed this morning. It was probably just as well that they kept their relationship on a strictly friendly footing, at least for the time being.

They ate breakfast together in friendly silence, until Richard said:

"I'll get those cards if you like, Enid, and some stamps if there's anything you need to do here."

"Well, the place could stand a good going over with the vacuum and a dust round," Enid said, getting up. "Do you want lunch here? There's enough food to last us several days and we shouldn't waste it."

"Fine, if you don't mind cooking it," he agreed. "Right, that stationery shop will be open now — I'll go. Is there anything else, Enid?"

"Could you get the local paper? It

comes out today. There might just be a job in it."

"OK, we can but look."

He dropped a quick kiss on her cheek and was gone, and she dealt with the soiled breakfast things, then got out her vacuum cleaner. She was just plugging it in when she heard footsteps outside, and straightened up, listening. It sounded as though someone was going up to Richard's flat, and she went to the door and opened it, just in time to see the back of a tall, slender girl disappearing round the bend in the stairs.

There was something familiar about that erect back and long slim legs, and with a sudden shock Enid realised that it was Gina.

What could she want? Enid wondered, hesitating, and then she heard Richard's doorbell and guessed that Gina had rung it, which must mean that she wanted to talk to Richard. *Now* what do I do? Enid thought, as the bell sounded again — speak to her, tell her what's happened, or dive back inside and pretend I've gone deaf? It might be better to tell Gina what had happened, or would Richard prefer to tell Gina himself, or maybe he wouldn't want to talk to her at all?

"Excuse me." Gina re-appeared and came down the stairs. "You're Enid, aren't you? You don't happen to know where Richard is, do you?"

"Yes, as a matter of fact, I do." There seemed no point in lying. "He's gone out to — to get some things for us both."

"Oh," Gina frowned a little, creasing her white brow. "When will he be back?"

"About half an hour, I should think, unless he has to wait for — " she stopped before 'the invitation cards' came out. "Can I do anything for you?"

Gina hesitated, then smiled a little.

"I would rather have given him this myself but I'm sure I can trust you," she said, opening her handbag. "It — it's my engagement ring, I came to return it personally."

"I see." Enid took the little envelope. "All right, I'll give it to him. Thanks, Gina."

She made to step back inside and close her door, but Gina was looking at her oddly, still frowning a little.

"You don't seem surprised," she said. "Did Richard tell you the engagement was off?"

"Yes. Yes, he did." Enid felt suddenly acutely uncomfortable. Should she invite Gina in or not? "I — I was sorry."

"Yes. Well, it seemed the best thing to do, in the circumstances." Gina smiled briefly. "I'd better go, you will give him the ring, won't you?"

"Yes, of course. Is — is there any message?"

"No, I don't think so, except good luck." Gina said, smiling again. "Goodbye, Enid."

She turned and went, and Enid went inside and closed the door, the little packet clasped in her hand. All Richard's dreams returned unfulfilled, she thought, then suddenly, she wondered why Gina hadn't simply returned the ring by post. Surely she hadn't come to turn the knife in the wound? Probably not, perhaps she'd felt that something so valuable should be given back personally, just as she had said.

"If I were a genuine fiancée in love with Richard I'd be furious with Gina for turning up here," Enid thought, but she wasn't in love with Richard so she wasn't furious, just a little curious as to Gina's motives.

Enid put the little packet down on the coffee table and returned to her cleaning, and a few minutes later Richard came back, the local newspaper rolled up under his arms. He was taking the invitation cards out of his pocket when Enid told him that she had seen Gina, and he paused, staring at her, his face curiously expressionless. Enid was reminded of a wall or a thick unmoving curtain, then he asked quietly:

"What did she want?"

"To give you back her ring." Enid handed him the packet. "She wanted to return it personally."

"I see." He frowned slightly. "You didn't tell her we were living together now?"

"No. I just said you'd gone shopping to get some things for us both. She said she could trust me and handed over the ring."

"OK. Maybe it's better that you didn't tell her. In any case it's none of her business now."

"What — what will you do with it?"

His lips took on a cynical line.

"Sell it back to the jeweller for as much as I can get," he said. "I — we can use the money."

"Yes. Yes, it might be best. Would you like some coffee?"

He nodded, the frown back again. Then he looked across at her with a smile.

64

"Enid, you should have a ring, shouldn't you? Not this one, but one of your own."

"Oh no, Richard, that's not necessary," she protested quickly. "Thanks, but it isn't — especially as we're both still hard up."

"Wait a minute," he said, and vanished into the bedroom.

Puzzled, she went into the kitchen to make some coffee, and when she came back he was holding something in his hand.

"Try it on," he said, and she took it with a faint smile.

It was a small, almost plain little ring with one blue stone. She slipped it over her finger, and to her astonishment it fitted. She looked enquiringly at Richard, and he said:

"It belonged to an aunt of mine and she gave it to Penny. Penny didn't want it and she gave it to me, thinking I might want to give it to Gina, but she wanted something a bit more showy. Is it all right for the time being?"

"Yes, it's fine and it really fits. Maybe that's a good omen. Thanks, Richard."

"Shall we write the invitation cards?" he suggested, and she nodded.

"The sooner the better," she said. "It shouldn't take long."

"You're right there," he agreed, grinning. "Enid, do we *really* want the Hatherleys? That woman's such a bitch."

"I know, but Mr Hatherley's an old friend, and he's really nice." She smiled. "I don't think Polly will make a scene, if that's what you're worried about."

"All right." He gave in gracefully. "Coffee first and then we'll do the cards. I bought some stamps while I was out."

★ ★ ★

Enid discovered that Penny and her husband David lived locally, in a new house just outside the town, and as she sealed the envelope for Richard she wondered what Penny would think when she discovered that her brother wasn't marrying Gina but a different girl altogether, one that Penny had probably never heard of. She put this tentatively to Richard, but he didn't seem perturbed.

"Whatever she thinks she'll keep quiet, and so will David," he said positively. "They're both very tactful."

"Do you think I should meet them before the wedding?" Enid suggested, and Richard considered this, frowning.

"Yes, I think you should," he agreed. "I'll ring Penny up later and see what her reaction is, but I'm sure they'll agree."

He went out to post the cards, and Enid prepared lunch, wondering apprehensively what Penny would think. She knew the terms of her mother's will, she probably knew how much Richard needed the money, so she would probably jump to the obvious conclusion. Would she be upset or sympathetic? Enid sincerely hoped the latter . . .

And what about Richard's father? They couldn't possibly hope to keep things secret from him, even if Penny and David didn't tell him, and that seemed unlikely, the news would filter through to him somehow, and then what would he do? What could he do? He had already thrown Richard out of the house so what was there left? Attempt to stop Richard inheriting his mother's money? But to do that he would have to prove that Richard's marriage was a sham, and how could anyone do that?

Richard came back smiling, then he looked searchingly at Enid and his face changed.

"Something wrong?" he enquired, and she told him what she had been thinking.

"I don't think you need worry," he said. "Penny's too fond of me to want to mess things up, and Dad has washed his hands. He wouldn't demean himself by having anything more to do with me, or so he said."

"Well, that's a relief," Enid said sarcastically. "I hope you don't mind salad because that's what we've got."

"Anything so long as it's food," Richard said hungrily. "I'm starving. It looks good, anyway."

He rang Penny that afternoon and left a message on her ansafone, grimacing slightly.

"I hate those things," he remarked to Enid as he hung up. "I feel as if I'm talking to a wall. Any luck?"

She looked up from the 'situations vacant' in the local paper and shook her head.

"Not really," she said. "I think I might have to look further afield for a job, there's nothing much here."

"M'm." Richard rubbed his nose thoughtfully. "Would it be better to wait until after the wedding, do you think? Have a break? You look as if you could use one."

"You may be right." She folded the

paper and stood up. "What do you want to do now?"

"Go for a walk?" he suggested. "It's stopped raining."

"Why not? I'll get my coat."

By mutual consent they walked towards the park, holding hands and talking, and Enid thought they must look like the average engaged couple. She had put the little ring on, and it felt a little strange, as if it really had no right to be there. But as Richard said, it would look queer if he hadn't given her one, and as they were trying to appear normal . . .

Richard had returned Gina's ring to the shop that morning, and Enid decided not to refer to the subject again unless he did. She sensed that Richard was still deeply disturbed by what had happened, and that any reference to it might be like probing a deep, raw wound.

They circled round the lake, and Richard started to discuss the plot of a new novel he had been planning for some time. She listened, oddly flattered that he was prepared to discuss his work with her, but when she said so he stopped walking and stared at her for a moment, one eyebrow climbing his forehead.

"Why feel flattered?" he said, grinning. "You're an intelligent girl, I like talking things over with you. I — I *like* you, Enid."

He slid his arm companionably round her shoulders, and she was totally unprepared for the warm, sweet feeling which swept unexpectedly through her. She blushed, tried not to, smiled, and stammered into speech.

"I — I like you too, Richard," she said. "Very much."

"Good." He gave her a hard, quick hug, and they walked on, past the children's playground, the bowling greens and the tennis courts, while Enid mentally composed herself.

It was too soon for anything more than liking, she decided, and yielding to physical attraction could be dangerous in this situation — and so very easy . . .

"I wonder if Penny's been trying to get in touch?" she said aloud, and Richard said:

"It's more likely to be this evening, Enid — she works."

"Oh. Yes, I suppose she does. Who for?"

"Dad, of course." This time his grin was totally without humour. "As I said, she's a bright girl."

Penny had obviously taken after her father, Enid thought — was Richard more like his scatty, romantic mother? She put the idea to Richard, and he considered it, his head slightly on one side.

"You're probably right," he said eventually. "And Mum was talented in her own way — she used to write for children, quite successfully. Incidentally, she and Dad got on very well."

Yes, but obviously what was acceptable in a wife wasn't acceptable in a son,

Enid thought, and began to dislike Richard's father, he sounded like a real autocrat. It would serve him right if Richard became a really famous author, a household name, in fact. She said so to Richard, and he laughed.

"That would be great," he said. "Then what should I do? Graciously forgive him?"

"After he'd *crawled*."

"That would be the day."

They left the park, still holding hands, and walked home slowly in the evening sunshine. The sun was going down in a deep pink sky, it was going to be a fine day tomorrow.

As Richard had predicted, Penny rang that evening, and Enid stood unashamedly listening to the conversation, a potato masher in her hand.

"Yes, of course, we'd love to, Pen," Richard was saying. "Tomorrow evening? Fine. Seven o'clock? OK. My best to David — yes, maybe you'd better tell Dad, then get ready to run for it — all right, all right, so you can manage him, stop bragging . . . bye."

He hung up, frowning and smiling at the same time, and turned to Enid.

"We're invited to dinner tomorrow," he told her. "She's bursting with curiosity and wants to meet you right away."

"Ow," Enid said, and Richard said quickly:

"You don't need to worry about Penny, Enid — just be yourself, she'll like you, they both will."

"Did she like Gina?" Enid asked, and Richard hesitated.

"Funnily enough, I suspect she didn't," he said thoughtfully. "Not that she ever said anything, it was just a feeling I had. Now you come to mention it, she didn't seem unduly surprised that Gina had walked out on me. Strange, that."

"Perhaps she'd heard something about Gina and Jo Marsh," Enid suggested tentatively, and Richard shrugged.

"Could be, I suppose," he said, and

abruptly changed the subject. "Dinner smells good."

Well, if he wasn't worried about his sister and her husband, why should I be? Enid thought as she went back to the kitchen. But all the same she was going to be extremely careful what she said tomorrow evening, and Richard should be too.

★ ★ ★

The next day Richard called at the garage where his car was being repaired, and came back with it, looking relieved. He came into the flat exclaiming:

"Thank God for that! I'd have hated to have to walk to Penny's, and taxis cost the earth."

"Is it all right now?" Enid asked, and Richard shrugged.

"Just about, but I do need a new one," he said. "They told me at the garage it was holding together from force of habit."

Enid laughed.

"Well, it'll do for now, won't it?" she said. "Richard, what shall I wear for tonight? I mean, do they dress for dinner or what?"

"Not when it's family, just wear a decent dress," he advised. Then he walked over and took her gently by the shoulders. "Not nervous, are you?"

"A bit," she admitted.

"Then don't be," he said gently. "Penny won't eat you, in fact I think you'll get along very well."

"I hope so." Unconsciously, she turned the little ring on her finger. "It's just that I feel you've had enough trouble from your family already, Richard."

"Not from Penny," said Richard, tweaking Enid's nose very gently. "So stop worrying."

All the same, as they drove up to the house and parked outside it, Enid's stomach felt as if a flight of lively butterflies had taken over inside it, and as they stood outside in the porch and Richard rang the bell, she clutched his hand for moral support.

Then the door opened and a tall, attractive girl stood there, smiling a welcome. She had auburn hair and brown eyes, and Enid would have recognised her as Richard's sister even if no one had told her.

"Richard, come in!" Penny exclaimed. Then her gaze switched to Enid, and her welcoming smile broadened.

"You must be Enid," she said. "David, they're here, darling."

A fair haired man appeared in the hall, smiling also, and held out a welcoming hand.

"Nice to see you both," he said. "Let me take your coat, Enid. Have we got time for drinks before dinner, Penny?"

"Yes, of course, darling, but it won't be long. Will you excuse me? There's something I should go and stir."

She grinned and vanished, and Enid, walking into a warm spacious lounge ahead of Richard, drew a deep breath of relief. Penny and David seemed

77

genuinely pleased to see them, and as she sank into a comfortable chair and looked round the room, she felt instantly at home. There were flowers and cushions everywhere, old oil paintings on the ivory coloured walls, and a tabby cat lay curled up asleep on the hearth rug. She bent over and tickled its ear, and it gave a friendly little purr, wriggled, and went on sleeping.

"That's Lizzie," David told her. "She does wake up occasionally. What would you like, Enid? Sweet sherry, or something stronger?"

"Sherry would be fine, thanks."

"Dry for you, Richard?" David asked, and Richard nodded.

As she took the glass from David, Enid's gaze fell on a corner china cabinet, and she went over to look at it.

"You've got some nice things in here," she commented, and David looked pleased.

"We chose them together," he said.

"I'm glad you approve."

"Enid's quite an expert," Richard explained. "Aren't you, darling?"

"It is my job," she said. "I love the shepherdess, David — is there a shepherd to go with her?"

"No, unfortunately, he's gone missing."

"Perhaps he eloped with a wood nymph," Richard suggested, and David grinned.

"Perhaps, but I think somebody probably dropped him," he said gravely. "Do you know anything about pictures, Enid?"

She was standing in front of one of the landscapes when Penny came back, announcing that dinner was ready.

"It's only a casserole," she said apologetically. "My Mrs Harper put it in the oven for us before she left. It should be tasty, though, she's a wonderful cook."

Helping herself to vegetables, Enid looked quickly round the large dining room. More old polished furniture, more beautiful pictures on the walls, a wonderful Chinese carpet lying in front of the fireplace . . . there was money here, and it had been very tastefully spent. She thought of her bare little flat with a sudden pang — Richard had noticed that her china had gone, but it hadn't been only the china — chairs, a Regency table, all sold to pay her father's debts . . .

"This is very nice, Penny," she said aloud, and Penny smiled.

"It's nice having you," she said with obvious sincerity. "Richard, if it's not a terribly tactless question — "

" — it probably will be, but go on," Richard said, in resigned tones.

"Who *did* Gina throw you over for?"

"Someone called Jo Marsh. I'd never heard of him," Richard said shortly.

"Jo Marsh," David paused, fork in hand, frowning. "That rings a bell somewhere . . . no, I can't think. Maybe it'll come to me later."

"Have you heard of him?" Enid

asked Penny, curiously, and she shook her head.

"No, the name means nothing to me," she said quietly. "Let's talk about something else . . . Enid, I believe you know about antiques, there's a brooch I'd like you to see. Maybe you can tell me if it really is what the jeweller said it is."

"I'll try," Enid promised, and silence fell for a few minutes.

David still looked puzzled, and occasionally he frowned, but Jo Marsh wasn't mentioned again, and Enid was grateful for it. After dinner Penny produced the brooch, and Enid was able to confirm that it was early Victorian and that the garnets and pearls were real.

"Good, I loved it when I saw it in the shop," Penny said, smiling. "If everyone's finished their coffee, would you like to see the house, Enid?"

"I'd love to," Enid said sincerely, and David grinned.

"What Penny really means is that she

wants a jolly good gossip," he said, and Penny smiled.

"What's wrong with that?" she challenged. "Come on, Enid — we'll have drinks when we come down."

Following Penny up the wide expensively carpeted stairs, Enid thought that this wasn't the ordeal she had envisaged — Penny and David were just as Richard had described them, and when Penny turned abruptly at the top of the stairs and smiled at her, she smiled back.

"Perhaps I shouldn't say this," Penny said, quietly. "But I'm glad Gina's gone — I never felt she was right for Richard — too ambitious. I know you don't equate nursing with ambition, but . . . I think you and Richard will get along just fine."

"I hope so," Enid said. "We've known each other for over a year now."

"M'm," Penny nodded, then threw open the nearest door and switched on the light. "This is our room."

"It's lovely," Enid exclaimed. "This is a beautiful house, Penny."

"We like it," Penny said. "We — we thought it was a nice place to bring up children, when the time came. It's a pity it's too dark to show you the garden, I'm very proud of that."

"Another time," Enid smiled. "Do you have a gardener?"

To her surprise Penny shook her head.

"Only very occasionally," she said. "It's David's weekend hobby, and I like gardening too. What do you think of the colour scheme in this bathroom? David thought I might have gone over the top but I think it's come off, don't you?"

"Yes, I do," Enid looked round slowly. "I like that little daisy frieze."

They went downstairs again, and if either Penny or David suspected a conspiracy between Richard and Enid, they said nothing, and Enid relaxed and enjoyed the rest of the evening. Only one thing happened to mar her pleasure. Perhaps unwisely, Richard asked how his father had taken the news of his approaching marriage, and Penny grinned ruefully.

"Loudly," she said. "At the top of his voice, in fact."

"Oh well," Richard said, shrugging. "What did I expect?"

They said goodbye to Penny and David at eleven, and as they were driving home, fairly slowly because Richard didn't want to push his old car, he said:

"Well, that was OK, wasn't it?"

"Yes, you were quite right about them," Enid said. "They're great, both of them."

"I knew Penny would like you," Richard said, slipping his hand over hers and squeezing it. "Did she say anything interesting when she took you upstairs?"

"Only that she wasn't very keen on Gina. She thought she was too ambitious."

"She could have been right at that,"

Richard said, after a moment. "Now I come to think about it, she probably was . . . Gina was always trying to make me stop writing, in a — a very quiet, subtle way, of course."

And then she would probably have worked on Richard to do as his father wanted, Enid thought with unusual cynicism . . .

"I — I'm quite glad she's gone," she said aloud, and Richard said:

"To be honest, so am I."

4

ENID took the dress she was wearing for her wedding out of the wardrobe and studied it critically. It was just right, she decided — a soft, deep yellow, and Richard had persuaded her to buy a matching coat and hat. Her small bouquet of cream and yellow carnations lay on the dressing table, and Richard's red carnation buttonhole lay beside it, waiting for its owner to calm down sufficiently to put it on.

He was standing beside Enid, staring at himself in the mirror and trying to make his unruly red hair lie down flat, which so far it had stubbornly refused to do.

"Damn it!" he exploded. "I knew I should have had a haircut! Enid, we should be leaving soon, can you hurry up?"

She slipped the dress over her head and it fell in silky folds to her knees. Richard zipped up the back, then stepped back to survey her.

"You look great," he said. "Can you help me with this buttonhole? I've jabbed myself with the pin twice."

She obliged, and Richard looked critically at himself again, fiddling nervously with his shirt cuffs.

"You look perfectly all right," she said soothingly. "That suit is really nice, and there's nothing wrong with your hair. I like it like that."

She wriggled into her coat, carefully put on her hat, looked at herself again, and turned to Richard. He seemed more tense than she did, but he smiled warmly at her and picked up his car keys.

"Shall we go?" he said. "We don't want to be late and I'm still not happy about that old banger of mine. It would be just our luck for it to go on strike halfway to the Registry Office, I wouldn't put that past it."

"Neither would I," Enid agreed, and picked up her bouquet.

The car started without complaint, however, and they started towards the Registry Office, not saying very much. Enid wondered how Mrs Hatherley would behave — correctly, she hoped, because even Mrs Hatherley wouldn't make a scene before witnesses. Mr Hatherley must have persuaded her to come, Enid thought, and she grinned wryly to herself.

Penny and David were going to be there, too, and Enid wondered again if there had been a stand up fight with Richard's father about this. However, Penny and her husband *were* coming, and so were two friends of Richard's from his college days, Bob Prentiss and his wife. Not very many people, but enough for a respectable looking wedding party and the buffet lunch afterwards.

"Well, here we are," Richard said, guiding the car into the car park and turning off the engine. "Ready, Enid?"

"M'm," she nodded, and they got out of the car and looked each other over critically before making their way slowly towards the front of the building.

As they turned the corner they saw Penny and David talking to a young couple, while Mr and Mrs Hatherley stood slightly apart, Mrs Hatherley with a faintly mulish expression and Mr Hatherley with a carefully blank face. It broke into a beaming smile when he saw Enid, and seconds later they were all greeting each other, and Bob Prentiss was exclaiming:

"Caught at last, eh, Rick? Or did you catch her?"

"Funny guy," Richard grinned. "Hello, Anne, I see you haven't managed to make him behave yet."

"I've given him up as a bad job" she said, laughing. "Hello, Enid, how are you? You look *gorgeous*."

"Well, thank you," Enid smiled back. Then her gaze switched to the Hatherleys, and she exclaimed: "I'm so glad you could come!"

Mrs Hatherley smiled frigidly, and the party moved slowly up the impressive steps and into the building.

Perhaps fortunately they did not have long to wait, and as she and Richard stood together to be married, Enid fought down a sudden feeling of intense panic. But it was too late now — the decision had been made, and she glanced sideways at Richard, half hoping for reassurance. She got a tight little smile in return, but his hand reached out and his fingers curled into hers, and suddenly her confidence returned and she made her responses quietly but clearly. Richard did the same, and in a surprisingly short time it was over and they were all outside, talking at the tops of their voices, hugging each other.

"Great!" Penny exclaimed, kissing Enid. Then, under her breath she whispered: "The best of luck, pet, and don't worry about Dad — he'll come round in time, I just know it."

"I do hope so," Enid whispered

back. "For everyone's sake."

Mr Hatherley kissed her, Mrs Hatherley kissed the air two inches from her cheek, Bob hugged her exuberantly, then produced a camera and took pictures, while Penny and David did the same, turn and turn about to make sure everyone had been photographed.

Eventually they all left for the restaurant and the buffet lunch, and Enid made up her mind that she might as well enjoy it — nobody had asked awkward questions, even Mrs Hatherley seemed to be unbending, she actually smiled at David. Bob was great fun and so was Anne. Richard had stopped fidgetting with his collar and cuffs and was laughing with Penny, the food was good and the waitress was sporting a buttonhole, smiling all over her face . . .

The party broke up at four, reluctantly, and when they went back to the car park they found that someone had painted 'Just Married' in several places on their car, and balloons of every colour adorned it. Richard looked at Enid, grinning and shaking his head.

"I bet that was Bob," he said. "Darn him, how on earth am I to get it off?"

"Don't worry about it," Enid said, smiling. "We're lucky he just put that and not something really ribald."

"Suppose so," Richard acknowledged. "Enid, are you tired?"

"Not really." She felt a little surprised at the question. "Why?"

"Because I've booked theatre seats for this evening," he said, grinning. "Not in London, in Redford. We've got time to go home and change first. OK?"

"Great!" Enid agreed enthusiastically. "It's ages since I've been to the theatre."

"Glad you approve," he said, climbing into his seat with a grunt. "Let's get going then, shall we?"

They hurried back to the flat, and it seemed to Enid, foolishly perhaps, that it should look somehow different, as if the events of the afternoon had changed it in some way. But it was just the same — tidy but a little bare, and she pulled a small face at the shabby lounge curtains before she followed Richard into the bedroom to change.

"I think it all went quite well, don't you?" Richard's voice was muffled as he struggled into his old familiar sweater.

Suddenly he stopped, looking across at Enid.

"You don't mind me wearing this, do you?" he asked. "I feel comfortable in it."

"Fine by me," she agreed, and reached for a pair of flat heeled shoes rather than the higher heeled patent leather pair she had intended to wear — it might look odd if Richard was casually dressed and she wasn't.

Richard sat down on the nearest bed — Enid's — and heaved a long sigh.

"I don't think anyone had any suspicious thoughts, do you?" he asked,

93

and Enid shook her head.

"No, I don't, and anyway, it doesn't matter. We're married."

"Yes," he looked at her thoughtfully. "Yes, we're married. How does it feel? To you, I mean?"

"Rather nice." She smiled at him, keeping her tone carefully light. "How does it feel to you?"

He stuck both thumbs in the air, grinning, then suddenly reached up and pulled her into his arms, giving her a bone cracking hug.

"You looked wonderful today," he said, his voice slightly husky. "I felt really proud of you."

"Thanks," she said, and a wave of unexpected feeling flooded through her, warm and exciting — and potentially dangerous . . . If Richard had kissed her then she would have returned his kiss with unrestrained passion, but as it was he let her go, gently and possibly reluctantly.

"Are you ready, then?" he asked. "I think maybe we'd better take a train, it'd take me too long to clean off the old banger."

"All right, if you've got the fare," she said, and he nodded ruefully, then his face brightened.

"At least I'll have some money soon," he said, standing up and reaching for his jacket. "OK?"

It was fortunate that the station was only a few streets away, Enid thought, as they stepped into the evening air, sharper now and with a hint of rain. Suddenly she shivered, and Richard, glancing at her with concern, said:

"Come on, let's walk briskly — doesn't the temperature go down when the sun goes?"

They stepped it out, but suddenly and unexpectedly, Richard's stride faltered, and she saw that he was peering at a shop front, and peered too, puzzled. 'Opening soon', a notice plastered across the window said, and a newly painted caption over the door said 'Sullivan Antiques'.

"That's new," Richard exclaimed.

"Enid, I wonder . . . "

"So do I." Enid exchanged quick glances with him. "There's nothing in the window yet — I wonder when they're going to open and how we get in touch with them?"

"How soon is soon?" Richard said, still staring. "We could find out, I suppose. What's the actual street number? Twenty nine . . . right, we'll check that out. Now we'd better get going."

They caught the appropriate train with minutes to spare, and as she flopped into a vacant seat Enid's mind went back to the new shop — 'Sullivan's Antiques'. Who was Sullivan, the owner or was it just a trade name? And was it going to be a genuine antique shop or just another place where they sold bric a brac or just plain junk? Either way it was worth investigating, and as quickly as possible.

★ ★ ★

They both enjoyed the play, a witty well acted comedy, and even the fact that it was raining when they left the theatre failed to depress them. Instead, they dived into a fish and chip shop for supper before catching the last train home.

"What a day!" Richard exclaimed as he untied his shoe laces and dropped his shoes on the carpet with a thud. "I'm beat. Enid, you have first go in the bathroom, I just want to sit here and go into a coma for a few minutes."

"You and me both."

Yawning, she complied, and when she returned he was almost asleep and she had to shake him awake. He padded off groaning, and she crawled into bed, pulling the duvet up under her chin. She didn't even hear Richard come to bed, pulling his own duvet up with a contented grunt.

★ ★ ★

When she awoke the next day his bed was empty, but he had left her a note. 'Gone to clean the car, back soon.' She got up, a curious feeling of disappointment assailing her. Somehow, she would have liked to see him before he went out, but the car did need cleaning so maybe it was as well to do it as quickly as possible.

He returned about an hour later, carrying a bucket and smiling triumphantly.

"Respectable at last!" he exclaimed. "Enid, what about that shop? I've had a thought — maybe the Job Centre know something."

"I already did, they're contacting the owner and getting back to me." She grinned smugly at him. "Want some breakfast?"

"Now you're talking," he said. "After which maybe I should go and do some writing."

"M'm," Enid nodded. "Sit down, then, I'll get it."

Enid was just swallowing the last of

her tea when the phone rang, and with a muttered 'excuse me' she went to answer it. Richard listened, his head on one side, and when she hung up he said:

"I can guess who that was. Do they want you to go and see whoever it is owns Sullivan's?"

"This afternoon at two thirty." Enid flopped back into her chair. "Wish me luck, we could use the money."

"Oh, I do, I do," Richard said, grinning. Then he became serious. "Enid, don't take it if it looks a dead end sort of job; you don't have to."

"I won't," she promised, and he leaned over and touched her hand briefly, as if giving her moral support.

★ ★ ★

Nevertheless, she felt extremely nervous as she approached the shop. She had taken care with her appearance, her hair shone with brushing, her make up was discreet, and she was wearing a honey coloured suit and matching blouse which Richard assured her looked terrific.

The shop door opened easily, and she stepped inside, looking round. Something was being done already — there were stands with various things on them, china of every description, two beautiful silver candlesticks, a rose bowl, and there were pictures on one wall. But the whole thing had an unfinished look, as if someone hadn't quite completed what they set out to do.

"Hello," Enid called, and a man appeared through a doorway at the back of the shop.

"Well hello there," he said, smiling, and Enid, who had expected someone middle aged and ordinary like Mr Hatherley, blinked.

This man was tall, broad shouldered and handsome, and when he came closer she saw that he had deep blue eyes, fringed with long dark curly eyelashes, and that his hair was dark too, thick and curling.

"Are you Mr Sullivan?" she asked, offering her hand.

"For the purpose of the business, yes," he said. "Actually I'm Jonathan Marsh. You must be — let me see, you've just got married, haven't you?"

"Yes, I'm Enid Cummings now."

"Sit down, Enid." He heaved two chairs forward. "I can't invite you into my office, it's an absolute tip, I've only just started getting things in order."

"Well, it looks fine so far," she said, and he smiled.

"I'm glad you approve," he said. "Now tell me about yourself. I understand you've been around antiques all your life."

She handed him her references and he read through them quietly, then gave them back with another smile.

"You seem very well qualified," he commented. "What I really want is someone like you to look after things when I'm not here, which I'm afraid will be quite often, this isn't my only business venture. I don't expect to make a profit just at first, by the way."

"Good, because I honestly don't think you will," Enid said quietly. "I'll do my best, of course. If you give me the job, that is," she added quickly, and his eyebrow quirked upwards, almost comically.

"Would you like it?" he asked, and she nodded.

"Yes, I think I would," she said. "You've got good things here, Mr — Mr Marsh, not junk. I don't think I'd be happy with too much of that."

"M'm," he nodded. "Just a little bit occasionally, eh?"

"Well, attractive junk," she conceded, and he laughed, showing very white, even teeth.

"When can you start?" he asked.

"Any time, really," she said. "When would you want me?"

"Tomorrow?" he suggested hopefully. "There's an auction I'd like to attend, perhaps we could go together."

"I'd like that," she exclaimed. "Where is it?"

"One of those big old fashioned houses on the Crombie road," he said. "I don't know if there'll be much worth having, but it might be worth while paying a visit, and as we're not officially open for a week or so we've got the time."

Enid nodded agreement, they discussed her salary, Jonathan apologised at not being able to offer her coffee, and she left, full of a bubbling sense of elation — she was working again!

Richard met her just outside the flat door, peered at her, grinned, and said:

"Don't tell me, you've got the job!"

She grinned back and he swung her off her feet, hugging her.

"Great!" he exclaimed. "Come on in and tell me all about it — want some tea?"

They sat opposite each other and she described the shop, while Richard nodded approval.

"Sounds fantastic," he said, reaching for another biscuit. "What's his name?"

"It isn't Sullivan, though he does look Irish now I think about it," Enid said. "You know, blue eyes and very dark hair — his name's Jonathan Marsh, and this isn't his only interest, so I'll be in charge most of the time — Richard, what is it?"

He had stopped, biscuit in hand, and was staring at her.

"What did you say his name was?" he asked.

"Jonathan Marsh. Oh — *Richard*, Jo Marsh!"

"Yes," he nodded, licking his lips as if they were suddenly dry. "Yes, it — it's got to be, hasn't it? Money and other interests? It must be, Enid, it's too much of a coincidence."

"Richard, I — I'm dreadfully sorry, I just didn't connect the two." She stared at him, full of contrition. "I'll tell him I can't take the job."

There was a long tense pause, then Richard shook his head.

"No," he said. "No, don't — don't do that."

"But Richard — " she stopped, then said: "Jo Marsh and *Gina* — surely you don't want anything to do with them?"

"Not socially, no." His smile was forced. "But the sort of job he's offering you, Enid, doesn't grow on trees. After all, I don't *have* to meet him, we can keep your job quite separate from everything else, can't we?"

"I — I suppose so, but — it could be awkward sometimes."

"Not if we behave like civilised people." This time his smile came more naturally. "It's over anyway, Gina and me — let's try to forget it, shall we?"

"That might not be too easy in the circumstances," she pointed out. "I mean, suppose he invites us out to dinner, what do we do then?"

"Find some reasonable excuse, I suppose." Richard was frowning again. "All right, Enid, maybe you do have a point . . . Listen, what I suggest is that you try the job for a month, maybe two or three, then if things are going smoothly you carry on with it. If they aren't — if it's too embarrassing — then you look round for something else. Does that sound logical?"

"Yes. Yes, it does. Richard, the last thing I want is for you to get hurt again."

"I know that." He leaned over and took her hands tightly in his. "But I've got to get Gina out of my system and it wouldn't be fair to stand in your way. Besides, I don't suppose you'd see much of her anyway, why should you? And Jo told you he had other interests, so you'll probably be very much in charge."

"You're probably right." Enid achieved a smile in turn. "Let's change the subject, shall we? How did the writing go?"

"Slowly." He released her hands and sat back in his chair with a sigh. "But I think it's coming."

"Good."

He showed her some of his work, and she read it carefully, but she found it difficult to concentrate. Jo Marsh's handsome assured face seemed to come between her and the printed page, and try as she would she still felt profoundly uneasy. Would she have felt the same if she and Richard had the usual sort of marriage? Probably much worse . . . and if Richard was really in love with her, would he want her anywhere near Jo Marsh or Gina, come to that? Probably not again . . .

★ ★ ★

But despite her qualms Enid enjoyed the next day. Jo drove rapidly and expertly to the house on the Crombie road and they arrived just as the auction was about to start. Enid recognised some of the faces around her, and whispered to Jo that there were quite a few dealers present as well as ordinary people who might be just curious or hoping to pick up a bargain.

"I'll let you decide what we bid for and how much," Jo said quietly, to her surprise. "I'm still a bit of a novice. Here, shall we look at the catalogue?"

They studied it together, and Enid began quietly ringing the items she felt were interesting, while Jo watched her, a half smile playing round his lips.

"You really know what you're doing, don't you?" he said.

"I hope so," she said, running an expert eye down the next page. "I don't think *that's* what they say it is . . ."

"You're the boss," Jo said. "Could we get a closer look at it?"

"The bidding's starting," Enid said, and mentally sprang to attention. "How much can we spend?"

"Whatever you think is reasonable."

"Right."

The bidding was fairly brisk, and though Enid lost two or three items, by the end of the morning she was fairly satisfied with her purchases. She stood with Jo while they were being expertly packed, and as they were placed carefully in the boot of Jo's large car she grinned triumphantly at him.

"I think that was worth the visit," she said, and Jo grinned back, sticking his thumb in the air.

"Let's go and have lunch somewhere, shall we?" he suggested. "Pub suit you?"

"Yes, but can we get this lot back to the shop first?" Enid said. "I don't want to leave them in a car park really, too many thieves around."

"OK." Jo opened the car door for her. "We'll do that."

They unpacked between them, carefully examining their purchases, while Enid mentally priced them.

"I don't think we'll make a fortune with these but they are nice," she said. "I love that little Christening mug, don't you?"

"I like the knives," Jo said blood thirstily "Warlike fellow the guy who

109

owned that house must have been . . . "

"I'll keep those locked up, I think," Enid said, flinching a little as Jo tentatively felt the thin blade with his finger. "They look sharp as razors."

"They are," Jo confirmed. "Now what about lunch? I'm starving."

They ate at 'The Pig and Gate', discussing their next move in a friendly way, and Enid thought that for a red hot businessman, if that was what Jo was, he was extremely approachable.

"Do you want to put price tags on them?" he asked, and Enid nodded.

"I'll do that this afternoon. Jo, do you mind telling me where you got your other things, the stuff you already had in the shop?"

"Most of it belonged to my mother," he said, reaching for his lager again. "She collected things. I kept the best of it, but there was so much left I thought why not start an antique shop? So I did."

"Why did you call it Sullivan's?"

"Sullivan was her maiden name," he

explained. "It seemed fitting, somehow."

"I see." Enid nodded. "Good idea."

"Let's hope so," Jo said, and drained his glass. "Let's get back to work, shall we?"

5

WHEN Enid reached home that evening Richard was out, but he had left a note propped against the clock, which said: 'Gone to library to verify something. Back soon. R.'

Suppressing a swift sensation of disappointment at his absence, Enid changed her clothes and started cooking, and a few minutes later she heard Richard's key turning in the lock.

"Hello," she called, and he came through to the kitchen.

"Hi," he said, kissing her quickly. "How was your day, then?"

"Pretty good," she smiled at him. "I'll tell you about it later — how was yours?"

"Better." He put several books down on the table. "The thing's starting to flow — it's really moving now. What's this Jo Marsh character like?"

"Well," Enid tilted her head to one side, thinking. "He's very good looking, he's easy to work with, and I think he's going to leave most of the buying and so on to me."

"Wise guy," Richard nodded. "Think you'll be happy, Enid?"

"I think so," she said cautiously. "It's early days, of course."

"Well, you don't have to stick it if you're not happy," Richard reiterated once more. "That smells good, by the way. Anything worth seeing on TV tonight?"

"I'm not sure, look in the paper and check."

They spent the evening comfortably relaxing in front of the set. If Richard had any lingering doubts about Enid's job he did not express them, and it wasn't until they were preparing for bed that he said, his back half turned to her:

"Do you think he — Jo, I mean — has realised who you are? That you're married to me, I mean?"

"I don't know," Enid said blankly. "Richard, I haven't the least idea if he has or hasn't made the connection."

"And you can't ask him," Richard squirmed into his pyjama trousers. "But if he doesn't I'll bet Gina will when he tells her about you." He grinned suddenly. "Wonder what she'll think?"

"If she's got any proper feeling at all," Enid said seriously. "She'll be glad for both of us."

"Yes, I guess so," Richard said, sober himself. He yawned. "I'm whacked, and so must you be. 'Night, Enid."

How was it, Enid wondered half an hour later, that you could be so tired and quite unable to sleep? She turned over in bed, listening to Richard's soft, even breathing, and thought grimly: 'At least he's happy.' And she should be too — she had a job which looked as if it could be interesting, a boss who appeared to be unexacting and pleasant to work for, her financial position was more stable than it had been for years, and she had Richard, a friendly and considerate companion . . . so why did she feel so uneasy again? Lying flat on her back now, she tried to rationalise her emotions. All right, she and Richard *weren't* in love, but they were good friends, and he appeared to be getting over Gina — or had he simply dismissed her from his mind, thrust her mentally away from him — trying to forget her, in other words . . .

And what about Jo Marsh? If he hadn't connected her with Richard and Gina, how long would it be before he did and would he mind? There seemed to be no logical reason why he should, but since when were human beings logical? Not that Jo Marsh had any right to complain, a man who had filched somebody else's fiancée from him . . . Should she casually draw Jo's attention to the situation, before Gina told him — if she told him . . . perhaps she wouldn't.

'I'll have to play it cool,' Enid thought. 'I won't say anything if Jo doesn't.'

She turned over again and resolutely closed her eyes.

In the morning her mood seemed to have changed. The sun was shining, Richard greeted her with a wide happy grin, and her night time uneasiness seemed stupid.

Richard had cooked breakfast, and they ate in companionable silence, Richard lost in creative thought and Enid mentally planning the day ahead. She wanted very badly to make a success of the shop, partly for her own satisfaction and partly for Jo's sake. Despite what he had done to Richard she liked him, even if that liking had a certain reserve and caution about it.

To her surprise he was there when she arrived at work, unpacking some brass candlesticks from an ancient cardboard box.

"Donated by a friend," he greeted

her with a smile. "Nice, aren't they?"

"Yes." Enid picked one up, nodding approvingly at its weight. "They could do with a clean, though."

"I'll do that," Jo said cheerfully. "Enid, can we open the shop today? Several people have had their noses stuck to the window. What about it?"

"I don't see why not," Enid agreed. "Are you going to be around for a bit?"

"Just for this morning," Jo said, picking up the candlesticks and walking into the back room with them. "OK, Enid, we're in business."

She turned the 'Closed' notice on the door round to 'Open', and a few minutes later their first customer appeared. She was looking for a birthday present for her mother, and went away with two matching china jugs, so obviously pleased with her purchase that Enid and Jo smiled at each other.

"There goes one happy lady," Jo remarked, dusting the place on the shelf where the jugs had been. "Shall we have some coffee on the strength of that, Enid?"

"I'll make it," she said quickly as the door swung open again.

The room at the rear of the shop served as a storeroom and small kitchen, with a cloakroom behind it, and as she made the coffee she could hear Jo talking to the customer. He had just the right manner, she decided, pleasant and friendly without being familiar, and in a way it was a pity that he couldn't be in the shop more frequently. She put the two coffee mugs on a tray with some biscuits and went back, just in time to see Jo deftly wrapping some silver teaspoons.

"Well done," she said when the customer had gone. "Do you take sugar?"

"One but no milk," he said, returning her smile. "Doing quite well, aren't we, so far?"

They continued to do quite well for the rest of the morning, and Enid put the notice round to 'Closed' with a feeling of reluctance.

"It seems almost a pity to waste time going to lunch," she remarked, as they left the shop together. "I'll get back as soon as I can, Jo."

"You take your proper lunch hour," he said firmly. "And have a proper lunch. I'll have to go now — I promised to meet my fiancée before I leave for London and I don't want to be late. 'Bye, Enid."

He grinned and walked away, and Enid wondered where he was entertaining Gina, not that it was her business, anyway. For a moment she toyed with the idea of going home herself, but it was a ten minute walk, and Richard might be concentrating hard, so she dismissed the idea and went into the first suitable looking cafe she saw. It was a relief to sit down, but she felt reasonably satisfied with her morning — it had been a good start.

★ ★ ★

The afternoon began slowly, and Enid was beginning to wonder if the morning's successes had been a flash in the pan when the door opened again and a woman came in. Enid opened her mouth to ask if she could help, then stopped halfway. The woman was Gina, beautifully dressed in a stylish coat and hat, her long slender legs adorned with sheer expensive looking stockings. For a moment she looked at Enid, then she smiled.

"It is you," she said. "When Jo told me your name was Cummings I didn't make the connection at first. Well, this is a surprise, Enid. I knew you and Richard had been friendly for a long time, but I didn't realise how friendly."

Enid stared at her, temporarily lost for words. Gina's tone was perfectly friendly, but the smile on her shapely lips had a faintly mocking little twist to it, and her deep blue eyes were mischievous. She *knows*, Enid thought or if she doesn't know, then she

120

guesses . . . Pulling herself together with an effort, she returned the smile.

"It's strange how things work out, isn't it?" she said innocently. "When I first saw the name Jonathan Marsh, I didn't realise that he was your — your new fiancé, Jo."

"Didn't you really?" Gina threw just enough surprise into her voice. "Does — does Richard know?"

"Oh, yes." Enid said, with a calm she was far from feeling. "But he feels like me, it's best to be sensible and civilised, don't you think so, Gina?"

"Yes. Yes, of course." If that wasn't the reply Gina had been hoping for, she didn't show it. "Much better for everybody. Jo told me you had a good morning."

"Yes, yes we did, better than I'd expected. I do want this venture to be a success."

"Well, now I'm here, may I look round?" Gina asked.

"Yes, of course you may, and if there's anything you want, I might

121

even give you a special price."

Gina laughed, showing beautiful even teeth, and Enid thought:

'She should have been a model.'

Then the door opened again, and with a muttered 'excuse me' to Gina, she moved forward to attend to the new customer.

All the time she was talking to the elderly gentleman, who was looking for a present for his wife, she was conscious of Gina moving quietly about the shop, picking up things and replacing them. The old gentleman took his time, eventually choosing a Chinese bowl, and as Enid wrapped it for him she sensed that Gina had found something she liked and was examining it closely.

"I like these," she said, holding out a delicately chased pair of nail scissors. "Do they work?"

"Oh yes, I tried them," Enid nodded. "They are pretty, aren't they?"

"Don't bother to wrap them," Gina said, producing a cheque book. "I'll put them in my handbag. Now I *must* go — give my regards to Richard, won't you?"

She handed the cheque to Enid with another dazzling smile and went, leaving a trace of expensive perfume lingering on the air.

Enid slipped the cheque into the drawer, and sat down for a moment on the stool behind the counter, breathing deeply. At least Gina hadn't started a row, though it would be difficult to discover grounds for one. After all, she had walked out on Richard, not vice versa . . . but all the same, Enid was thankful that she had gone.

The rest of the afternoon passed comparatively quietly. A steady stream of customers kept Enid busy until closing time, and as she carefully locked up and started to walk home she heaved a sigh of relief. So far, so good . . .

"Hi there, how's the working girl?" Richard greeted her. "Had a good day?"

"M'm." Enid tossed her handbag into the corner of the settee and wriggled out of her coat. "A very good morning, not such a busy afternoon. How about you?"

"Great," Richard said enthusiastically. "It's really going well, Enid. Want to go out for a meal or are you too tired?"

"Whatever you like," she returned his smile. "I know, get us a Chinese, but there's no hurry. Richard, there — there's something I should tell you."

"Yes?" he queried, his gaze suddenly intent, and she described Gina's visit.

"She wasn't nasty or anything like that," Enid said, while he listened quietly and without interrupting. "But I think she may have guessed things are — well, unusual."

"That doesn't matter," Richard said, his tone hard. "It's not her affair, is it? Just so long as she doesn't try to make trouble for you with Jo, in which case you leave at once. All right?"

His nostrils were pinched, and

indentations had appeared on each side of his nose — he looked angry, almost formidable, and Enid nodded silently. If Gina did interfere in the running of the shop, then she *would* leave, and she didn't need Richard to tell her.

"Right, then," Richard said. "That's that. I don't suppose you'll see much of her, Enid, why should you? There's no real reason why she should want to poke her nose in, after all."

"No, perhaps not." Enid was relieved to see his expression relaxing. "But I did think of something, Richard, and it may be silly, but what if they ask us to their wedding? What do we do then?"

"Well, go, I suppose." Richard's smile was lopsided. "But we'll meet that hurdle when we get to it. Now let's forget her, shall we? I'll go to that Chinese restaurant in the square. Tell me what you like and I'll get it."

She made a quick list, he shrugged himself into a coat and was gone, leaving her more dismayed than relieved. He had looked so angry — he wouldn't have looked like that if all his feelings for Gina had gone. Richard still cared for her, whatever he said or how hard he might try to dismiss her from his thoughts . . . and where did that leave her, Enid?

'I shouldn't have agreed to this,' she thought. 'It was stupid.'

But she had agreed, and now she must act the part, until enough time had elapsed to make their separation look like the breakdown of a normal marriage, not something contrived between them.

She went into the bathroom to freshen up quickly, knowing that there was very little she could do except stay on friendly terms with Richard, cause no gossip, and try to make the shop a success . . .

Richard came back with their dinner, and as if by mutual agreement they didn't discuss Gina or Jo. Richard talked about the plot for his new novel, listening carefully to the tentative suggestions Enid made. They sat for a long time over the bottle of wine he had bought, while he scribbled notes and argued about the plausibility of his plot.

"I don't think it's too far fetched, Richard," she said. "You read stranger things than that in the papers every day. Go ahead and write it."

"That's what I like about you," Richard said with his quick grin. "So positive . . . shall we have some coffee?"

★ ★ ★

Enid jerked awake, raised herself on her elbow, and stared across at Richard's bed. Yes, the moaning sounds were coming from him, and he was rolling and twisting, she could dimly see an arm threshing the air and a foot sticking out from under the duvet. The moaning got louder, then became words . . .

"No, no, no!" His voice rose to a

127

shriek, and Enid reached for the light switch, then slid out of bed.

"Richard, wake up! It's me, Enid — wake up, you've been having a nightmare." She grasped his shoulder and began to shake him gently. "It's all right, it was just a bad dream."

His eyes opened and he stared wildly at her, panting, then intelligence dawned in his face and he flopped back on his pillow, his arm across his forehead.

"Phew," he said, after a few seconds. "God, that was awful — Enid, I'm sorry — I woke you up, didn't I?"

His pyjama jacket was drenched with sweat, and his hair was damp. Enid sat down on the side of his bed and smiled reassuringly at him.

"Whatever were you dreaming about?" she asked, as matter of factly as she could. "It sounded as though a sabre toothed tiger was after you."

"Something sure was," Richard said. His breathing was slowly returning to normal, but instinctively she took his hand in hers. It felt clammy and it shook slightly, but after a moment or two it gripped hers tightly.

"Do you often have nightmares?" she asked, and he shook his head.

"No. I used to have them as a kid, though." He smiled shakily at her. "Funny thing, I can't remember what I was dreaming about."

"You can't always," Enid said comfortingly. "Richard, take off your pyjama top, it's soaking."

He sat up, and she put out her free hand to help him. As the damp jacket slid to the floor her hand touched his bare shoulder, and it was as if a sudden electric current flowed from it into her own body. Suddenly still and rigid, she looked at Richard, and as their eyes met he leaned forward, took her chin in his free hand, and kissed her — not the friendly, easy going kisses of the past, but a close, warm, intimate caress . . . her senses swam, her arms went round his neck and they clung together, until Richard pulled her gently into bed with him and heaved the duvet cover over both of them . . .

★ ★ ★

"Enid?" The tone was questioning, and her eyes opened reluctantly.

She looked straight into Richard's face. He was sitting on the edge of the bed, looking down at her, and he gave her a funny, half triumphant, half apologetic smile.

"Hi," he said. "Are you all right?"

"Yes. Yes, I think so. What — what time is it?"

"Just after seven. Want some tea?"

"No, no, not just yet." She thought he looked rather like a little boy not quite sure of a grown up's possible reaction. "You — you didn't have another nightmare?"

"No." He grinned suddenly, and this time triumph was uppermost on his face. "No, the rest of my dreams were terrific."

She bit back a smile and sat up.

"So were mine," she said demurely, and a laugh bubbled out of her. "Oh, Richard, what a start to making love!"

"Enid, you didn't mind, did you?" His eyes searched her face. "I didn't jump the gun, did I?"

"Of course not." Her hands came out and clasped his tightly. "We — we're married, aren't we?"

"Too true." He grinned. "Now let's have that tea."

He vanished in the direction of the kitchen, and Enid lay back on the pillow, remembering the night's events. They had embraced with real passion and tenderness, as if they were really in love . . . well, perhaps they were . . . or perhaps they *could* be . . .

Richard came back, hooking the bedroom door open with his bare foot, and Enid sat up again.

"Oooh! Chocolate biscuits!" she exclaimed. "Such extravagance!"

"Well, we're celebrating, aren't we?" he said, kissing her.

"M'm." She smiled back, happiness

swelling up inside her, and in that moment she knew beyond any doubt that whatever Richard's feelings for her might be, hers for him were the real, permanent thing . . .

"Watch it, I've overfilled the mug," Richard warned, and she took it cautiously.

"This is nice," she said. "Can we do something special tonight?"

"Why not?" He disposed of a biscuit in two bites. "Cinema? Dinner out? Name it."

"Dinner out, please."

"Right, I'll book us in somewhere." He yawned, grinned mischievously and said: "I think I'll have nightmares more often."

"No, don't, you sounded awful, really distressed," Enid said seriously. "Can you remember anything about it?"

"I dunno." He ran his hand through his thick tousled hair, frowning. "My father was in it somewhere, and I think Gina was there as well, and something seemed to have gone wrong with my word processor, but any other details — they've just gone."

"It doesn't matter," she said quickly. "You make good tea, Richard."

"I know." He smirked. "Actually — I never told you this, did I? — actually, I'm not a bad cook, either. My mother gave me a few lessons before I went to university — she thought it was a good idea, and she was right."

"So she could be practical sometimes," Enid commented.

"Yes, she could. She could manage Dad, too, and she was clever about it — he never realised he was being manipulated."

"Good for her," Enid said drily.

"Well, as the old adage has it, you catch more flies with honey than vinegar, don't you?" Richard grinned. He leaned over and kissed her again. "Is that the time? We'd better get up."

"Do you mind if I shower first?" she asked.

"No, you're the one who has to go

out first. You carry on, I'll make some toast."

She heard him whistling as she went into the shower, and smiled to herself. He was happy, probably happier than he had been for months, and their relationship was on a firm footing. There wouldn't be any more talk about separating. She grabbed the shower soap and began to sing contentedly to herself. Everything was fine . . .

6

ENID opened the shop a few minutes early, still in a daze of happiness. As she hung up her coat her mind went back to the night before, and she smiled to herself. Nobody could say now that she and Richard had married for convenience.

She heard the shop door open, then close, and jerking herself back to the present, she went to see who the customer was. To her surprise Jo Marsh was there, peeling off his scarf.

"Hello," she exclaimed. "I didn't expect to see you here."

"I came to see how you were getting on," he smiled. "You're looking very happy — something tells me you had a good day yesterday."

"Yes, I did." Unlocking the cash register, she said: "Just you look in there. By the way, Gina came in and bought some scissors."

"Oh, did she? I thought she might. She was really curious about you. What did she think of the place? I haven't seen her since yesterday lunch time."

"She seemed quite impressed," Enid said. "She had a good look round."

"Well, she has strict instructions to tell all her friends about it." Jo moved into the back room. "I can stay for an hour or two if that's any help."

"Yes, it would be. I suppose some of this money and the cheques ought to be banked today. Perhaps one of us could do that later."

It was fortunate that Jo had appeared, because the morning started off even more briskly than the previous one, and by lunch time Enid had taken several hundred pounds.

"Well, either we've caught on because you know what you're doing or because we're in the right location, or both," Jo said, as he turned the notice on the door round.

He seemed to have forgotten that he

had said he could only stay for an hour or two, and suggested a pub lunch. For a moment Enid hesitated, then as she couldn't think of a valid reason why not, nodded agreement.

"Shall we call at the bank on the way?" she suggested, but Jo shook his head.

"I'll do it this afternoon," he said, and once again, Enid felt surprised, but she fell into step with him.

He was about the same height as Richard but more heavily built, and there was an air of self-confidence about him which Richard didn't possess. When he was older he would have what her father used to refer to as 'a Presence' Enid thought, and smiled a little.

"Why the smile?" Jo asked suddenly. "You've been looking very happy all the morning."

"It's because everything's going so well," Enid said quickly. "I suppose I'm rather relieved."

"Me too, if I'm truthful," Jo said,

checking his stride and pushing open the pub door for her. "Antiques are a new venture for me. Want a drink before we eat?"

"No, thank you, but you have one if you like. It's nice and warm in here, isn't it?"

"It needs to be," Jo said feelingly. "I'm beginning to wonder if it's ever going to be Spring, it's taking so long to get here. Have a look at the menu, Enid, I'm going to get a beer."

She sat down at a table near the fire and picked up the menu, wondering if she should offer to pay for her own lunch. Jo came back with his drink.

"What are you having?" he asked. "I think I'll settle for a ploughman's."

"So will I," Enid said, and he went to the bar to order them.

When he came back Enid tentatively suggested she should pay for hers, but he said: "Rubbish, I asked you."

His tone was brusque but he softened it with a smile. It lit up his whole face, and suddenly Enid knew why

Gina had fallen in love with him — he was certainly a most attractive man.

They were halfway through their meal when they both became aware that someone was standing close by, and they looked up simultaneously to see Gina standing there with a surprised expression on her face.

"Hello, darling," she exclaimed to Jo. "I didn't expect to see you here. I thought you were going back to London."

"I was," Jo rose and pulled a chair back for her. "What would you like to eat?"

"Whatever you've been having," Gina said, sinking down gracefully. "But please hurry, I haven't got long."

"Right," Jo went to the bar, and Gina turned to Enid.

"Has he been in the shop all the morning?" she asked, her tone incredulous, and Enid nodded.

"He wouldn't go," she explained.

139

"We were terribly busy. If this keeps up maybe we should employ somebody else."

"It certainly sounds like it," Gina said. "If it isn't just a flash in the pan, of course."

"I certainly hope not," Enid said.

Although Gina's expression was quite friendly, Enid had the distinct impression that Gina wasn't too pleased at finding Jo and Enid together, even in a crowded pub at lunchtime.

Jo came back with Gina's lunch, which he placed before her with a smile. She said 'thank you', returning the smile briefly, and picked up her knife and fork.

"Excuse me if I don't say very much," she said. "I've got to be back at the hospital in about half an hour."

Silence fell, then Jo went for coffee, and Gina asked:

"How's Richard? How's the new novel coming along?"

"Very well," Enid replied. "He's fine and he's pleased with the novel so far.

I think it's good myself, the plot's unusual."

"Well, let's hope his editor likes it," Gina said. "Such a — a precarious profession, I always think."

"I suppose it is," Enid agreed. "But if everyone felt like that, nobody would ever write anything."

"That's true, I suppose," Gina acknowledged. She hesitated momentarily, then added: "His mother's money will be very useful, of course."

Enid glanced sharply at her, but Gina's pleasant expression stayed the same. 'Play it cool' Enid thought, 'she can't *know* anything.'

"Yes, it will," she said calmly. "I'm very glad he got it — I don't want to criticise his mother, but that really was a most peculiar will."

"Oh, I agree with you," Gina said, also calmly. "People really shouldn't be allowed to make wills like that — they really should be invalid."

"I believe in some countries they are," Enid said, and relief swept over her as Jo reappeared with three cups of coffee on a small tray.

"I've had to fight my way through the mob," he said, grinning. "Darling, it gets more crowded in here every day. I nearly dropped this lot twice."

"Perhaps we'd better find somewhere else, then," Gina said, her answering smile exclusively for Jo. "Oops, this is *hot*!"

"Can you make it back to the hospital in time?" Enid asked, and Gina nodded.

"Just about," she said. "I'll see you this evening, Jo."

"Yes, I'll call for you, usual time," he said, and Gina took another scalding sip, gathered up her handbag and stood up.

"I must go," she said. "Goodbye, darling."

Jo half rose, but she dropped a quick kiss on his forehead and went, swaying gracefully through the press and disappearing into the street.

"Gina says you should really be in

London," Enid said. "Have you missed any important appointments?"

"Nothing that can't be dealt with on the phone from the shop," he said. "Don't worry about it, Enid. Listen, do you think we should get someone else to help in the shop? You could interview them yourself."

"Can we wait until we're sure it's not just — we're not just a nine days wonder?" Enid said. "It would be silly to employ someone and then have to sack them again."

"Maybe you're right," Jo said. "OK, we'll see how it goes. Can you manage this afternoon? I really should be somewhere else."

"Yes, of course." Enid smiled. Then a thought struck her. "Jo, can you give me a phone number where I can reach you if necessary? I promise I won't use it unless I have to."

"Yes, of course, I should have thought of that myself." He took a card out of his pocket. "You'd better use my home number, I'm never in the same place twice during the day."

They parted outside the pub, and Enid opened the shop. A steady stream of customers appeared, and it was closing time before Enid realised it. She locked up, tired but satisfied, and walked home in the gathering dusk.

Richard greeted her with a hug, and when she asked how his writing was going he said 'Very well'.

"I think I'll look in on you one morning," he said, as Enid dropped into a chair with a sigh. "I'd like to see what you've done to the place."

"Yes, but it might be better to make sure Jo's not around first," Enid said, and Richard shot her a sharp look.

"Has he been around today?" he asked, a frown between his eyebrows.

"This morning, and it was just as well, we were frantically busy. He went to London this afternoon."

"H'm." Richard grunted. "Well, he's not afraid to get his hands dirty, that's something in his favour, I suppose. Did you have lunch together?"

"Yes, at a pub, and Gina walked in. She didn't say anything, but I don't think she was pleased."

"At seeing you two together? Serve her right," Richard said vindictively. Then he looked sharply at Enid again. "He hadn't — I mean, he hasn't made any passes at you, has he?"

"Oh no, nothing like that. I think Gina — well, I think maybe she's not so sure of him as she could be. Just a feeling I have."

"You could be right." Richard turned and headed for the kitchen. "I'll make some tea."

Enid leaned back in her chair, closing her eyes, smiling a little. There had been a definite note of jealousy in Richard's voice, as if he really cared. She could hear him moving around in the kitchen, but resisted the temptation to go and help. Her legs were tired, for one thing . . .

Richard came back with a tray, and Enid thankfully took her steaming mug.

"Ooh, I needed that," she exclaimed. "You do make *gorgeous* tea, darling."

"Well, thank you," Richard smirked. "Kind of you to say so."

They sipped in contented silence, then Richard told her that he had booked dinner at a restaurant in the town.

"Oh," Enid said, a little blankly. "That sounds nice, but — but can we afford it?"

"Just about, and I thought you should have a treat. The table's for seven-thirty, so there's plenty of time. Enid, at the risk of being a bore — you will tell me if that Marsh guy tries anything on, won't you? He sounds a bit of a fast worker to me and you don't have to put up with that."

"Yes, of course I will, but I'm sure he only thinks of me as a business colleague, Richard. I really think it's Gina for him."

"M'm. Let's hope you're right. Want to see what I've been doing today?"

She assented, and Richard produced his work. Enid read it with careful concentration, then looked up at him, nodding approval.

"That's fine," she said. "Go on like that and novel number two will be accepted before the summer's out."

"Let's hope so." He gathered up his papers and smiled down at her. "Toss you for who showers first."

During the next few days Enid settled her debt with the bank, Richard bought a new car, and the antique shop took on a feeling of prosperity. Enid was pleased, both for herself and for Jo, and Richard was becoming increasingly absorbed in his own work, so much so that Enid wasn't really surprised when he told her that he should go to London to do some research in one of the museums.

"It's quicker than writing to them," he explained. "I'll stay the night, I think — easier than coming back and going again the next day."

"Book somewhere beforehand," she

147

advised. "Then you won't waste time looking."

"Right." He nodded. "You will be OK without me, won't you?"

"Of course I will." She reached up to kiss him. "Take your time. Give me a ring if you're going to be longer than you thought."

"Will do." He returned the kiss, and the next day he left, and the flat felt curiously empty without him.

Enid went to work and was soon engrossed, until just before twelve there was a lull and she slipped into the back of the shop to make some coffee. Then, just as she sank into a chair with a sigh, she heard the shop bell ring, and heaved herself up again with a stifled groan . . .

She went back into the shop, smiling, and the tall, well built man standing there turned and looked at her. She looked back, and the smile froze at his expression. It was grim, and his gaze raked her from head to heels and back again. For a startled moment she thought he must be a dissatisfied customer, then realised that she had never seen him before. Yet there was something familiar about him, something about the nose and chin she half recognised.

"Good — good morning," she pulled herself together. "Can I help you?"

"I doubt it," he said, and his voice was as hard as his look. "I'm Richard's father."

'I should have known,' she thought. 'He's older and bigger, but Richard looks like him . . . '

"How do you do?" she said aloud, wondering if she should offer her hand, and deciding against it as his gaze travelled over her again.

"Well, you're a pretty little thing, there's nothing wrong with Richard's eyes whatever's the matter with his brain," Mr Cummings said, with devastating bluntness. "How did he get you to agree to marry him so soon after Gina? Was it the money? I heard you were in debt."

Enid gasped. Richard had warned her, but it hadn't prepared her for anything like this. Colour flamed in her face as anger came to her rescue.

"That's none of your business," she retorted. "Especially as you said you didn't want any more to do with him. What do you want, anyway? I haven't time to listen to abuse."

A glint of something which might have been appreciation appeared in his eyes for a moment, then vanished as his expression became grimmer than ever.

"You can give that son of mine a message from me," he said. "Tell him I'll give him one last chance. He can come back to where he should be, helping to run the firm, or that's *it*, I want nothing more to do with him."

"I rather think that's mutual," Enid retorted. "I'm afraid your firm will have to stagger on without him. Now if that's all I do have things to do."

Appreciation flashed in his eyes again for a split second, and she thought he was going to smile.

"Just tell him," he said. "I mean it."

"So does Richard," she said, giving him look for look. "He doesn't take kindly to being bullied and neither do I. Good morning, Mr Cummings."

He turned on his heel and left, almost colliding with someone coming in, and with a feeling of surprise she recognised Jo.

"Hello," she said, and to her annoyance her voice shook. "I didn't expect to see you."

Jo closed the door, looking searchingly at her.

"Who was that?" he asked quietly. "He seemed angry and I thought I heard raised voices."

"That was Richard's father," Enid could see no point in lying about it. "He came in to give me a message for Richard."

"I see. Now let me guess. Come back to the firm or all is over between us," Jo said with a smile. "I'm right, aren't I?"

151

She nodded, and Jo took her elbow and steered her gently into the back room.

"Let's have some coffee," he said. "You look as if you could do with a cup."

"I'd just made some," she said, but Jo threw it down the sink.

"Tepid," he said tersely. "You need something hot and strong and sweet. As I expect you've guessed, Gina told me about that will and the row Richard had with his father. I'm glad he stuck to his guns, it's stupid to try to make someone do something they don't want to, especially when they're someone as intelligent as Richard. I should have thought a man as experienced as Mr Cummings would know that."

"I guess he likes his own way," Enid said ruefully, and Jo grunted.

"So do we all," he said, measuring coffee into their mugs. "But we can't always have it, can we?"

He smiled at her, Irish blue eyes crinkling at the corners, and she felt his physical attraction like a blow. No wonder Gina had fallen for him, she thought . . .

"What are you going to tell Richard?" he asked suddenly, and Enid shrugged.

"The truth, I suppose," she said. "Not that it will make any difference, especially now."

He handed her the coffee, and she sipped it with a little grimace. It was too sweet, almost syrupy, but Jo said quietly:

"Drink it, you've had a shock. By the way, you didn't let him get away with it, did you?"

"I told him I didn't appreciate being bullied," she said, and surprised herself by grinning. "He looked quite surprised."

"Good." Jo grinned back. "The only way to deal with a man like that is to stand up to him. Feeling better?"

"M'm, thank you." She listened, then got up. "That was the doorbell, excuse me."

Jo stayed for another half hour, then

excused himself and left, and Enid
tried to put Richard's father firmly
out of her mind. He wasn't worth
worrying about, she told herself, he
was a tyrant and a bully, the sort of
man who bulldozed his way through
everything in his path and got vicious
if anyone stood up to him. Richard
had been perfectly right to behave as
he had. She picked up a duster and
started to clean a shelf, dismissing Mr
Cummings from her mind. Then, just
as the door opened again to admit
another customer, a disturbing thought
shot into her mind — she would have
to tell Richard what had happened but
how would he re-act to Jo knowing
as well?

★ ★ ★

Richard listened quietly to what she told
him, then reached over and covered her
hand with his.

"I'm sorry, darling," he said, running
his other hand through his hair. "That

was despicable of Dad, coming and having a go at you. I'm glad you told him what you thought. It's a pity Jo Marsh walked in just then, though."

"I don't think it told him anything he didn't know already," Enid said. "Gina told him about the row and the will. He said he was surprised your father didn't have more sense than to bully people like that. He was very nice, actually."

"Oh well." Richard shrugged. "Let's forget it, shall we? But if he — my father — tries that again, tell me at once and *I'll* settle him."

"I suppose," Enid said slowly, wrinkling her forehead. "I suppose it means that he — he still cares about you in a strange sort of way. I mean, if he didn't he wouldn't want you in the business, would he?"

Richard looked at her expressionlessly for a moment, then he nodded.

"You're probably right," he said, a rueful twist to his mouth. "But Enid, I just *can't* — if only he'd accept that, we would be — well, friends again, but he won't."

Enid's thoughts flashed to her own father. Ineffective dreamer though he had been, he would never have tried to impose his will on anyone . . . in that respect she had been luckier than Richard, much luckier.

"Richard," she said tentatively, groping for the right words. "Would you — do you think it would be a good idea if we invited your father to come here, for dinner or — or lunch, or — or something? He — he is your father."

Richard stared at her, then reached over and took her hand.

"Do you think that hasn't occurred to me?" he asked, smiling. "But it would serve no purpose, darling. He would simply take it as a sign that I was weakening and there would probably be another scene, and I've had enough of those to last me a lifetime. Dad never gives up an idea — he — he's like a bulldog with a bone, he never lets go!"

Enid laughed, and Richard pulled her into his arms.

"Let's forget him, darling," he whispered, fondling her. "We've got our own lives to lead . . ."

Perhaps he's right, Enid thought, as his lips explored hers hungrily — she pushed Richard's father firmly away from her thoughts and responded eagerly to Richard . . .

★ ★ ★

It was Gina who re-opened the subject. She appeared in the shop the next morning, bringing in a waft of expensive perfume. Enid turned to greet her, duster in one hand, a valuable plate in the other. She put it down carefully and smiled at Gina.

"Hello," she said. "Nice to see you — can I help you?"

Gina returned the smile, shaking her head.

"Thanks, but I didn't come to buy anything," she said. "I hope you won't

157

be offended, but Jo told me about Richard's father coming to see you yesterday, and I wondered — " she stopped, flushing faintly, and Enid wondered what was coming.

"Strictly speaking it's nothing to do with me," Gina said, after a pause. "But it does seem a terrible pity that — well, that things are as they are between them both."

"It is a pity," Enid said, pushing a chair in Gina's direction. "But there isn't anything I can do about it, Gina — I tried last night."

"Yes, I tried too." Gina sat down. "I truly did. The trouble is, they're both so *stubborn* — in different ways, of course."

"Perhaps they are." Enid leaned against the counter, thinking that maybe she should resent Gina, but she couldn't. Gina looked genuinely concerned, she was frowning and biting her lip.

"I suppose," Gina smoothed her glove with one finger. "I suppose it wouldn't be possible for Richard to — to work for his father and write in his spare time? That's just a suggestion, Enid."

"I don't think so." Enid ran her hand through her thick curly hair. "It might if Richard wasn't so dedicated to his work, but I think all that would happen is that his father would be so demanding he wouldn't get a chance to do any writing at all — I should imagine Mr Cummings is the sort of man who expects total concentration — a hundred and one percent, in fact."

"You're quite right," Gina said, smiling briefly. "It's just that I've known Richard's family for such a long time, Enid — I knew his mother and I know Penny. It seems so sad."

"It is sad in a way," Enid agreed. "But there doesn't seem to be anything we can do about it."

Silence fell, then Gina rose briskly to her feet.

"Thanks for not biting my head off,

Enid," she said. "I do wish you and Richard well, you know."

She smiled again and went, closing the shop door gently behind her, leaving Enid oddly shaken. Had Gina come from genuine concern or had she some ulterior motive? If so, it was difficult to see what it could be. Gina had nothing to gain or lose, whatever happened between Richard and his father.

* * *

That evening Enid repeated Gina's conversation to Richard, as accurately as she could remember it, and he listened, frowning.

"I see," he said. "I wonder now, did someone put her up to that?"

"I wondered too," Enid admitted. "But she did seem honestly worried, Richard."

"Gina always could act," Richard said, with a mirthless grin. "I think what we might be getting here is a two-pronged attack — Dad and Gina, damn her."

"We don't know that she was got at," Enid pointed out, and Richard wriggled his shoulders, as if he was trying to shed an irritating burden.

"No, we don't, but I bet I'm right," he said slowly, as if weighing his words. "Enid, I've been wondering — should we move, away from the district, I mean? We're too close to my father and old associations for my liking. After all, there are other pleasant places and we could afford it."

Taken completely by surprise, she stared open mouthed at him, and he grinned crookedly.

"Oh, I know we agreed to stay here, but we're not getting much peace, are we? First Dad and now Gina. If we cleared out at least we could have a fresh start."

"I don't know what to say, Richard." Enid found her voice. "I've never really thought about moving."

"Well, think about it now," Richard

said, with a forced smile. "Then we'll discuss it again."

Enid nodded without speaking, while a strange foreboding grew stronger and stronger inside her . . .

7

ENID lay awake for some time that night, thinking over what Richard had said. Was he right? Would it be better to make a fresh start somewhere, away from their old memories and associations? Her common sense told her it might be, but there were other things to consider — where to go, for instance, and how long it would take them to sell the flat, unpredictable at the best of times. And what about her own job? She was really enjoying it, where would she find another one like it? And what about Jo? Didn't he deserve a little consideration, especially after the chance he had given her? Jobs like hers weren't easy to find, as she knew to her cost, she could be out of work for months, and although their financial circumstances were better, they couldn't afford that.

But if Richard wasn't happy, if his father was determined to go on harassing him, then perhaps he was right, a complete change might be better. At least Mr Cummings wouldn't be able to reach them so easily, especially if they were careful not to let too many people know where they were going.

She turned over in bed, listening to Richard's breathing. It was calm and even, but she had a feeling that he wasn't asleep, but was lying awake like herself, his thoughts turning this way and that . . . raising herself slightly on her elbow, she whispered:

"Richard, are you awake?"

"Yes, I am," he whispered back. "Can't you sleep either?"

"No," she reached over and switched on the bedside lamp. "I keep thinking about what you said."

Richard sat up in bed, dragging his pillows behind his head and shoulders, and Enid did the same.

"I'm sorry to spring it on you like

that," Richard said, smiling his crooked smile. "But it all seems such a mess — Dad, Gina, even you working for Jo Marsh — I know you're enjoying it, but there are other jobs, you'd find one, Enid. Dad won't leave us alone, darling, I know he won't."

He looked suddenly forlorn, like a lost boy, and she leaned over and took his hand, holding it tightly in hers.

"All right, darling," she said gently. "We'll do it, but you realise that your father will find out we're moving and may try to find out where we're going."

"I realise that," Richard said. "There'll be 'For Sale' notices outside, for one thing. Unless . . . "

"Unless what?"

"Unless we rent the flat out to somebody instead."

Enid considered this for a moment, then shook her head.

"He could still find out," she said. "There would be 'To Let' notices instead."

"M'm," Richard frowned, then shrugged. "You're right . . . but if we tell the estate agents not to reveal our new address, that might stop him."

"Only if we don't let it slip to anyone here," Enid said slowly. "Especially not to Jo or — or Gina."

"Especially not to them," Richard said, his mouth suddenly grim, and then Enid exclaimed:

"What about Penny and David, Richard? You can't keep your own sister in ignorance."

"Some people do," he muttered, then his rueful smile reappeared. "You're absolutely right, of course. It would be very difficult, but at least we'd be away from here."

Enid nodded. Richard's memories must be very bitter. It could be that it were those he was trying to escape from, as well as his father's ominous nearness.

"All right," she said, speaking in a deliberately matter of fact tone. "Will you go and see some estate agents? It

166

would be easier for you than me."

"Yes, I'll do it tomorrow — today, rather, it's past midnight."

"But before you go, have you any idea where you want to move *to*?"

"Several ideas." Richard smiled naturally for the first time. "Listen, why don't you think about it and we'll discuss it tom — I mean, tonight. Remember, we can go anywhere we like."

"How about somewhere abroad?" she asked tentatively, and he looked startled, as though that idea hadn't occurred to him.

"That's a possibility," he said slowly. "Yes, we'll talk about that, too."

"If Jo appears do I tell him?" Enid asked, and Richard gnawed his lip, then shook his head.

"Not until the notice goes up," he said. "He might sack you on the spot."

"He might at that," Enid said. "Perhaps I should offer to train somebody else before I go."

"M'm," Richard nodded. "Yes, you could do that, I suppose. Shall we try and get some sleep now, darling?"

"Yes, we should."

She put the light out and wriggled into a comfortable position, and eventually sleep came.

★ ★ ★

Perhaps it was as well that Jo didn't appear at all on the following day, as Enid's thoughts were in a turmoil. Were they doing the right thing? It could take months, even a year to sell the flat, and at the thought of being in a state of indecision for as long as that Enid felt almost panicky. There would be all sorts of people tramping round the flat, disturbing their quiet, criticising, curious, some of them genuine and some of them simply nosey . . . did Richard realise what he was letting himself in for? She had a feeling he didn't . . . and suppose it disturbed his writing, as well it might?

As if to answer her unspoken question, the telephone rang and it was Richard.

"I won't keep you long, darling," he said, and his voice sounded almost jubilant. "I've done it, I'll give you the details when I see you tonight."

"Oh." Whatever she had been thinking, it was too late to say anything now, Enid thought. "That — that's good."

"Just thought I'd let you know," Richard said, and hung up.

That's that, Enid thought, and went slowly back into the shop, where two teenage girls were looking for a present for their mother. Finally they chose a Japanese vase, and as she wrapped it carefully for them, Enid wondered mildly where on earth they'd got all that money — weekend jobs, perhaps? They left, chattering and happy, and a shabby middle aged man came in, carrying a bag with some miniatures in it he wanted a quick valuation on before he sold them. Enid gave her opinion and he thanked her gravely, then left without telling her who his prospective buyer was or offering to pay for the valuation.

Her mind went back to the sale of the flat, and she was still deep in thought when the door opened again and Jo came in, tugging off his scarf and exclaiming about the cold.

"Hello," Enid said. "I didn't expect to see you today."

"I'm taking some time off," he said, smiling. "How's things?"

"Not so bad," Enid returned the smile. "Want some coffee?"

"Sounds good," Jo said. "When is this weather going to change?"

"Don't know." Enid led the way into the back room, filled the kettle, got out the mugs and the milk, and turned to face him. "It's a pain, isn't it?"

He was looking at her, frowning slightly, a puzzled expression on his face, and to her annoyance she felt herself flushing slightly.

"Is anything wrong, Enid?" he asked.

"You don't look happy."

"Well, you may as well know now," Enid said. "Richard has put our flat on the market."

There was a long pause, then Jo said slowly, in a curiously expressionless tone:

"I see. Why did he do that? Was it something to do with his father?"

Enid nodded.

"He just wants to get away from here," she said. "He feels his father won't let him alone until he gives in and goes to work for him."

"What do *you* think?" Jo asked, his blue eyes intent. "Are you in favour of this move?"

"Well," Enid said, reaching for the now steaming kettle. "I can see his point and maybe he's right. Mr Cummings is very persistent."

"Mr Cummings is a pain in the backside," Jo said forthrightly. "But sometimes, Enid, you have to live with a pain. Where would you go, anyway, has he thought about that yet?"

"We're thinking it over," Enid said. Then, impulsively, she added: "Jo, I am sorry, but I'll stay as long as I can, and I'll train someone else for you if you like."

"Don't worry about that," Jo said quietly, "I'm more concerned about you. Selling and buying property is no easy matter these days. It could take months, maybe even longer."

"I know, and that's what's bothering me," Enid said. Once she told Jo about the flat, the rest of the story came out quite easily. "I don't think Richard realises that there'll be people to view, and places we must see, and all sorts of irritations he hasn't thought of yet, and I wouldn't be surprised if his father comes and makes a frightful scene when he finds out what we're doing, and he will find out, I'm sure of that. Either someone will tell him or he'll see the notice board."

"And scenes bother you, don't they?" Jo said, smiling. "I'm sure you'll cope with Mr Cummings if he does try anything like that. Enid, he can't touch you, not in any way. Richard must be almost financially independent, and he's held out against his father this long, he can do it for a bit longer, I'm sure. I think he's got more guts than perhaps you've given him credit for having. Maybe this move is right for both of you."

"Maybe." Feeling better, she smiled back at him. "Thanks for the pep talk, Jo, I feel better now."

"Good." He slipped his arm round her and gave her a quick, hard hug. "Hello, is that the door?"

"I'll go," Enid said, and went into the shop . . . Then her polite: "Can I help you?" died unspoken as Polly Hatherley marched over to her, glaring:

"Yes, I might have guessed it was you," she exclaimed, venomously. "It's always *you*, isn't it?"

"What's the matter?" Enid asked, astonished, and Mrs Hatherley said:

"Miniatures, that's what's the matter, and your stupid valuation on them.

We were going to buy them from that — that stubborn old fool, but he had to come to you first and you — you overvalued them by *hundreds*! Who do you think you are, anyway?"

Conscious of movement behind her, Enid recovered herself.

"Mrs Hatherley, I didn't know you were that gentleman's prospective buyers, and those miniatures are beautiful — I don't think I overvalued them, but he can always go and get another opinion, can't he? He doesn't have to accept mine, and neither do you."

"Oh, *I* don't," Mrs Hatherley said, red angry spots burning in her cheeks. "But he does, and he's taken them elsewhere, and we had a customer who was very keen to have them, too. Why can't you mind your own business?"

"Excuse me," Jo said, moving up to stand at Enid's elbow. "But Mrs Cummings has every right to give an opinion if she's asked for one, and she's probably right. She's very

174

knowledgeable you know."

Mrs Hatherley's gaze travelled from Enid's startled face to Jo's calm one, and her eyes narrowed.

"Who are you?" she demanded. "Another one of her — " she stopped, and Enid wondered what she had been going to say. "Who are you?"

"I'm Jo Marsh, the owner of this shop," Jo said, taking Enid's elbow in a tight, comforting grip. "How do you do."

"I'd do a great deal better if someone would do something about this — this *girl*," Mrs Hatherley almost spat. "She's a menace. Did she tell you about the valuable vase she broke? No? I thought not."

"Mrs Hatherley, *please*!" Enid cried, and with a final glare, Mrs Hatherley turned on her heel and flounced out, banging the door behind her with a resounding crash.

"*Wow!*" Jo exclaimed. "Who was *that*?"

"Polly Hatherley," Enid's voice shook.

"I used to work for her husband."

"Well may the saints watch over the poor man," Jo said, in a stage Irish accent. "Because he must need their intercession . . . What was all that about, Enid? Come on, sit down and tell me."

She was glad to sink into a chair, her knees felt wobbly and she was near to tears. Jo let go of her elbow with reluctance, then made some more coffee while Enid told him about the vase, Mrs Hatherley's behaviour, and the shabby man with the miniatures.

"I didn't mean to upset a deal they were making, Jo," she said. "He didn't say anything about the Hatherleys, just that he wanted a valuation before he sold them."

"Just as well he asked you," Jo said drily, thoughtfully scrunching a biscuit. "It sounds to me as though they were getting ready to cheat him and you put a stop to it."

"It sounds like that to me, too," Enid said reluctantly. "Or maybe it was just

Polly — she's quite unscrupulous, you know."

"So I gathered," Jo said drily. "Are you all right now?"

"Yes, thanks," Enid nodded gratefully. "I'm sorry about all that, Jo — Polly can't stand the sight of me and I suppose when my name came up she just exploded."

"You could put it like that," Jo said, drily again. "A very volatile lady."

"M'm." Enid managed a smile. "Thanks for standing up for me, Jo."

"No problem," Jo said easily, his eyes crinkling at the corners. "But Enid, tell me one thing, if indeed you can — *why* does she dislike you so much? Is it just chemistry or is there a real, valid reason?"

"Richard — Richard thinks she's jealous about me and Mr Hatherley." Colour came and went in Enid's face. "And it's stupid, Jo, there's nothing for her to be jealous *about*."

"M'm, I thought it might be something like that." Jo took another biscuit. "But then, you are a very attractive girl, Enid."

His gaze, blue and intent, was on her face and she blushed again. Jo started to say something, and then Enid heard the doorbell and with a muttered 'excuse me' hurried into the shop.

Enid half expected an apologetic Mr Hatherley to appear sometime during the afternoon, but he didn't, and she was glad of it. She felt that the less she saw of the Hatherleys the better — Polly was a nuisance, suppose the shop had been full of customers when she had burst in? Would she have made a scene then? The answer to that was probably 'yes!' An audience would have spurred her on.

Jo left at about four, telling her not to worry about Mrs Hatherley or the proposed house-moving.

"It will be OK, I'm sure of it," he said, winding his scarf round his neck. "You've got my home number if you need it? Good, you can leave a message on the ansafone if necessary."

He smiled and went, and Enid turned back to the customer she was serving, thinking she was lucky to have Jo for a boss. Kind, easy going, supportive . . . she would miss him when she left.

Richard was waiting for her eagerly, and greeted her with a bone cracking hug.

"Did you see the 'For Sale' board?" he asked, when he finally released her. "They don't waste much time, do they?"

Enid, who had seen it with mixed feelings, nodded.

"What happened?" she asked.

"Someone came round from their office and looked over the flat," Richard said. "He said it was in very good decorative condition and so on, that he would arrange for viewing by appointment only, and he left these brochures of other properties all over the place for us to look at, and see if anything takes our eyes. They've got other branches, you see, so they can do that. We'll have a look later, shall we?"

"They sound very efficient," Enid said, easing off her coat, and Richard gathered it up, grinning at her. Then his expression changed.

"Is anything wrong?" he asked. "You look tired out. Did something happen?"

"Polly Hatherley happened," Enid said, sitting down. "Want to hear about it?"

"I guess so," Richard said, with a groan of resignation, and she told him.

"Oh my God!" Richard said, disgusted. "So you unwittingly stopped them cheating somebody, or so it would appear — you *were* sure about those miniatures, were you?"

"Pretty sure, and I made it clear it was only my opinion." Enid stretched wearily. "He was quite free to go and get another one if he wanted."

"Apparently he was quite happy with yours," Richard said. "And so am I. What a pain that woman is!"

"Yes. To be honest, I was quite glad Jo was there. He stuck up for me nobly." Enid forced a smile. "Darling, can we just forget it and have something to eat?"

"Of course we can. I've got us spaghetti bolognaise."

"I thought something smelled nice."

"I hope it is. No, sit still, I'll do it."

Enid sat looking round the room. Would she be sorry to leave? Like Richard, she had good memories and painful ones, but whereas in her case good memories predominated, in Richard's the painful ones must be paramount. He was obviously relieved to have done something positive. She could hear him singing in the kitchen, something he had never done before, and her lips curved in a tender smile. What did it matter where they lived so long as they were happy?

Richard re-appeared with two steaming plates, and she pushed her doubting thoughts away and joined him at the table.

They spent most of the evening poring over the brochures the estate agent had given them, and deciding on a plan of campaign.

"The best thing to do is pick a few of the likelier looking places and visit them in turn," Richard suggested. "It would have to be at the weekends, of course, unless you can get away sometimes in the week. By the way, how did Jo react to your news about the move?"

"He seemed to think it might be a good idea," Enid said. "But he did point out it might take a while."

"Well, we know that," Richard grinned. "Gives us longer to decide where we want to go. Now, how about this place? I like the look of it."

Enid looked in her turn.

"It seems great," she said. "The trouble is, it's difficult to tell from the blurb, and the photographs can be deceptive, too. But I agree with you, it does seem nice. Where is Biddlehurst?"

"Sussex, I think. Tell you what, I'll let them — the agents — know we're interested, and see if they can fix us up with an appointment. How's that?"

"Fine. Better try and make it at the weekend, and make sure nobody wants to come and look at this place, we don't want to miss a prospective buyer," Enid said. "Oh, I suppose the agents do all that — the arranging, I mean."

"That's what they're for," Richard said, grinning again and reaching for her hand. "Happy, darling?"

"M'm." She returned his kiss. "Of course I am."

"How about an early night?" he suggested softly, and she nodded agreement.

"And by the way," she said with mock severity as they rose to go. "Did you do *any* work at all today?"

"Yes I did," Richard said indignantly. "And it's going very well, thank you."

"Well, all right then," Enid said. "But I'm surprised you found the time."

"So was I, to be honest," Richard said, suddenly sober. "I'll have to keep at it, Enid, and not be too distracted by what's going on."

If he realised that then one of her fears was laid to rest, Enid thought — maybe if the house in Biddlehurst was suitable, they could buy it, and the whole thing would be over more quickly than she thought it would be . . .

It was Jo who called Enid's attention to an antiques auction a few miles away, and when she apologised for somehow missing it he told her he'd had inside information.

"Can we go?" he asked. "I know it would mean shutting the shop for a morning, but it might be worth it. What do you think?"

"You could be right," Enid said, running her eyes critically down the list of things for sale. "I know this house, there could be something really worth having. All right, I'll put a notice up on the door. I expect it will be all over by mid-day, there isn't that much stuff to go. Can you spare the time to come with me?"

"Yes, and I'll drive," he said. "We'd better start early so that you can take a look at things and get some idea if they're the genuine article and so on."

"Yes, I must do that," Enid agreed, and two days later they set out, Enid still glancing at the catalogue and wondering if the Spanish chest was genuine seventeenth century or a copy. It looked authentic from the photograph, but she wanted to look all the same.

They must have been about two miles from their destination when Jo's car began to complain, and he looked at the dashboard and groaned.

"Enid, I'm a fool!" he exclaimed. "We're in the red — I meant to fill up yesterday evening and I forgot. Wait, there's some petrol in the boot."

He got out, and Enid bit her lip. They were tight for time, and any hold up would make them tighter. Jo reappeared with the can, heaved up the car bonnet, poured the petrol into the tank, replaced the bonnet and put the can back in the boot.

"Sorry about that," he said apologetically. "I'll fill up if we see a garage on the way."

He started the car, and Enid crossed her fingers . . .

It was almost ten o'clock when Jo parked the car outside the large impressive old house, and Enid hastily unclipped her seat belt and got out of the car.

"We must hurry," she said, and then she saw someone waving furiously at her from the wide steps. "Now who — oh, it can't be!"

"Someone you know?" Jo enquired, and Enid nodded.

"It's Charlie Appleby, an old friend of Dad's, I haven't seen him for

186

months. Jo, would you mind going in and standing in for me if they start the bidding? I won't be long."

"Right." Jo went up the steps three at a time and disappeared into the building, and Charlie advanced on Enid with open arms, beaming.

"Lovely to see you!" he exclaimed. "How are you? You're looking very well. Who was that handsome fellow you were with? Your husband?"

"No, my boss." She returned Charlie's hug. "But I am married, I'm Mrs Cummings now. Hadn't we better go in? They'll be starting soon."

"I suppose so." Charlie fell into step with her. "Enid, that chest — they've moved it to first lot, *don't* touch it. I've had a look and I'm sure it's a fake, a good one but still a fake. Oh, lord, they've started."

They had, and to her horror Enid spotted Jo, catalogue in hand, apparently bidding five hundred for the chest. She tried to catch his eye, but the auction room was crowded, and he was watching the auctioneer. The bidding rose sharply and she shut her eyes in anguish. Two thousand, then three, three thousand five hundred . . . then Jo turned his head and saw her. She shook her head furiously, mouthing 'no!' He looked startled, but he shrugged and turned away, making his way quietly over to them.

"I'm sorry, Jo," she whispered. "But Charlie says it's a fake so I had to stop you. Charlie, this is Jo Marsh, my boss."

"Nice of you to warn us," Jo said in a low voice. "Hello, I think it's gone — who's the unfortunate new owner?"

"It's Polly Hatherley," Charlie said, equally muted. "I didn't get the chance to warn her. Not," he grinned wickedly "that I would have, I can't stand the woman. Foul tempered and a know it all to boot. Do her good to get her fingers burned."

"Well, I'm glad it wasn't us," Jo said. "Are you going to bid for the candlesticks, Enid?"

"Go ahead, they're nice and I'm not interested in them," Charlie smiled. "It's those Georgian chairs I'm after for a client."

Enid secured the candlesticks for a reasonable price, then a small Regency bureau and some spoons. There was nothing else she wanted, but Jo bought a small clock and they watched the rest of the bidding. Then, suddenly, Enid realised that Polly was staring at them, her eyes narrowed and her lips tight, and Enid recognised that look. Polly was furiously angry, but why? Jo noticed her as well, and whispered:

"What's wrong with that woman now? She looks as if she could bite us in half."

"I thought that was her usual expression," Charlie said, pulling a face. "The one she generally wears."

Enid giggled, Jo grinned, and Polly's cold stare became a ferocious glare. Then, with a toss of her head, she turned her back on them.

"Charming," Charlie muttered. "God help her husband. There, it's over — shall we collect our ill gotten gains and go?"

They loaded their purchases carefully into the back of Jo's large car and left, and as they drove away Jo remarked:

"Charlie seems a nice guy — was he right about that chest, do you think?"

"M'm, he's an expert on old furniture, and an old friend of Dad's, that's why he warned us." Enid smiled suddenly. "I wonder what Polly will say when she finds out that chest's a fake?"

"Sell it on to some unsuspecting idiot, I expect," Jo said unsympathetically. "She wouldn't have believed Charlie if he had told her, anyway."

"Probably not," Enid agreed, and let the matter drop.

★ ★ ★

But she told Richard when they met in the evening, and he laughed.

190

"Serve her right," he said unkindly. "She must have looked before she bought it, surely."

"Maybe, I don't know. How have you been getting on?"

"Not so bad," he leaned over and kissed the tip of her nose. "Someone came to look at the flat this morning, but I don't think they'll take it. They've got children and wanted a garden. I couldn't make out why they were looking in the first place, it seemed odd. Curiosity, I suppose. Enid, I think I'll have to go down to London tomorrow, do you mind? There's something else I need to verify."

"All right," she said. "Will you let the estate agents know? We don't want someone coming here for nothing."

"I already did," Richard said, with an air of smug efficiency. "No interested viewers until after the weekend."

That seemed to be that, and Enid gave herself up to enjoying the evening. Richard was in very good spirits, and when he whisked her off to bed his love making reflected his mood. They fell asleep pressed closely together, and Enid's last thought was that theirs was a proper marriage now . . .

8

IT was Richard who got up first the next morning, appearing with a mug of tea for Enid and a happy grin.

"You won't believe this, but the sun's shining," he said in tones of exaggerated awe. "I stuck my head outside and it's almost *warm*."

"Thank goodness for that!" Enid took the mug with a smile. "Maybe it really is Spring at last. Thanks, darling."

"I'm going for a shower," he said. "It's early, stay where you are for a bit longer if you want to."

Enid sipped her tea blissfully, then slid out of bed and went into the kitchen to prepare breakfast. Richard came out, rubbing his tousled hair and humming tunelessly under his breath, and she ached with love for him.

"Can I have two eggs?" he asked hopefully, and she nodded.

He had been right about the sunshine, it was streaming in through the window, lighting up the room and striking brighter colour from the daffodils Enid had arranged in a vase on the small table. He sighed contentedly, grinned at her and sat down, so obviously at peace with himself and his world that she smiled back sympathetically. He reached for her hand and held it for a moment, releasing it reluctantly to reach for some toast, and they ate in companionable silence.

Enid had a quiet but profitable day, with no irate Polly or difficult customers, and there was no sign of Jo, but she didn't expect him. He had told her he was going to London, and had a date with Gina in the evening, and she suspected that he might have been neglecting his other interests to be in the shop. She locked up carefully, walked home and spent a quiet evening catching up with odd jobs and reading.

Richard rang and told her that he was staying away for another night and to expect him when he appeared.

"All right, darling, stay away as long as you must," she said. "See you soon."

He said goodbye and hung up, and she decided on an early night.

★ ★ ★

The next day was even warmer than the previous one, and as Enid walked to work she was conscious of rising spirits and a sense of well being. A bird was singing loudly in someone's back garden, and she smiled. He would soon be nesting and raising a tuneful little family of his own, and a sudden thought came unbidden into her mind. How did Richard feel about children? Did he want them, and if so, how many and how soon? That was something she would have to ask him when the time seemed right . . .

As if the sunshine had brought people

out, she had a very busy morning, and it was with a sigh of relief that she turned the notice on the shop door and went into the back room for her coat and handbag. Then, as she started to lock up, she saw Jo striding along the pavement towards her, and paused, key in hand.

"Enid, can we go inside?" he said, and she stared at him, her eyes widening.

"Yes, of course," she said. "Is something wrong?"

He followed her into the shop, locking the door behind them.

"You were just going out to lunch, weren't you?" he said. "I'll ring for some sandwiches and coffee if that's all right."

"Yes, of course it is. Jo, *is* something wrong? You look — upset."

"I am. Just a minute, I'll get our food organised."

He picked up the phone and with his usual crispness ordered a packed lunch, then hung up and turned to face her with an almost apologetic smile.

"Sorry about this," he said, pushing a chair in her direction. "I think you'd better sit down, Enid, this isn't going to be easy."

Apprehensive and bewildered, she sat down on the edge of the chair, managed a wavering smile, and waited.

Jo seated himself opposite her, sighed sharply, and said:

"This is going to sound disloyal to Gina, but you've got to know. We had dinner last night, and a flaming, really ugly row — not just a tiff, a horrendous quarrel."

"But what about?" Enid asked, more bewildered than ever.

"About you, mainly." He smiled but it was a strained, painful effort. "I'll try and begin at the beginning, shall I?"

"It might be a help," Enid said, returning the smile. "I won't interrupt."

"It appears that our mutual friend Polly invited Gina out to lunch yesterday and put in the poison about you — about us — in no uncertain manner. They knew each other because Polly was in hospital a few months ago, met Gina and they made friends. Gina likes antiques so that was a bond between them, and that's how Polly knew that Gina and I were engaged — they kept in touch."

"Yes, I see. Did you know they knew each other?"

"No, not until last night." Jo ran his hand through his hair, and she thought how tired and strained he looked. "Polly told Gina her version of the vase incident, the affair of the miniatures, and also told Gina that we were working together to force up the price of that chest — which by the way *is* a fake, Polly got someone to verify it."

"For heaven's sake!" Enid said. "Working together? What nonsense!"

"Apparently Polly told Gina I did the bidding, forced the price way up, then dropped out when you caught my eye and told me to, thereby making Polly pay well over the top for the damned thing."

"But there were other people bidding too, didn't you tell Gina that?"

"You bet I did, but Polly had somehow convinced her that you and I did it for spite — told her we were laughing together about it with 'that awful Charlie Appleby', and we *were* laughing, Enid, I had to admit that."

"But not because we were doing *that*," Enid said. "I'm surprised Gina believed her, honestly — Jo, I think that's our lunch."

He got up and went to the door, and Enid sat back in her chair, her thoughts racing. There was more to come, she was sure of it — something much more personal and serious, Jo wouldn't have been so anxious to talk to her if it had only been a question of Polly's tantrums. She could hear a muffled conversation going on at the door, then it closed and Jo came back, carrying a neat cardboard box and a flask.

"I'll do it," Enid said quickly, and

he watched while she poured steaming coffee and opened the sandwich box.

He took one and bit into it, and Enid did the same, but she got the impression that he hardly knew what he was eating, and her apprehension grew. Finally she said:

"Jo, there's more, isn't there? Please, tell me."

"All right. Gina thinks, thanks to something Polly said, that you and I are having an affair, and she is threatening to tell Richard."

Enid gasped, closing her eyes for a brief minute, then she took a long deep breath.

"Didn't you deny it?" she asked, and Jo smiled crookedly.

"Of course I did, until I was blue in the face. God, Polly must have a real way with words, I've never seen Gina so upset, it was like talking to a brick wall."

"Jo, this is *awful*," Enid said, after a long pause. "What are we going to do? Are you — are you still engaged?"

"For the life of me I'm not sure," Jo said, and this time his smile looked more natural. "I think it's hanging by a thread."

Enid was silent, unable to think of anything to say. She put down the uneaten portion of her sandwich, while the implications of what Jo had told her sank in. Would Gina carry out her threat, and if she did would Richard believe her or not? Enid had no way of knowing, and there was no way of stopping Gina, absolutely none.

"What are we going to do?" she asked finally, and Jo shrugged his shoulders.

"I haven't the remotest idea," he said, with endearing frankness. "We could wait and hope Gina cools down. I could murder Polly."

"Don't do that," Enid forced another smile. "We'd be in worse trouble than ever."

Jo took a long swig of coffee, choked, spluttered, and apologised, then looked at Enid and asked:

"What are *you* going to do? Tell

Richard what's happened? It might be best in the long run."

"Richard's in London tonight and possibly tomorrow, verifying something for his new novel," Enid said. "But you're right — it's better for him to hear it from me than Gina. Jo,I really am sorry about all this — that *wretched* woman!"

"I don't think I've ever met anyone quite so spiteful," Jo said simply. "And I've been about a bit, I can tell you."

"Would it be better if I left the shop?" Enid suggested. "Then at least Gina won't feel we're working together."

Jo considered this, then shook his head.

"Why the devil should you when you've done nothing wrong?" he said, and there was a real undercurrent of anger in his voice. "And where would I get anyone to replace you at such short notice? And where would you get another comparable job around here? You could be out of work for months. It could take a year for you and Richard to sell the flat and get somewhere else to live. No, I'm damned if I'll dance to that Polly's tune. I love Gina but there are limits. If she doesn't trust me, well, that's up to her. I've told the truth, the ball's in her court. But do tell Richard what's happened, Enid, before Gina gets to him, because at the moment she's likely to say anything, true or false."

"Is it worth while talking to Polly?" Enid suggested tentatively, and saw white indentations appear round Jo's nostrils and mouth.

"I couldn't trust myself," he said. "And what's the point, the damage is done."

It was, and Enid reached for her mug of cooling coffee and forced some of it down.

"Thank you for telling me, Jo," she said. "It can't have been easy. I — I seem to have brought you nothing but trouble."

"Now don't you be saying things like that," Jo exclaimed. "It's not your fault that woman's got her claws in you and I wish I could do something to stop her. Unfortunately it's not a criminal offence to have a poisonous tongue."

"When are you seeing Gina again?" Enid asked, and Jo shrugged.

"Up to her," he said, and there was a hard set to his jaw. "She knows where to find me when she's ready to apologise."

"Ooops," Enid said before she could stop herself, and an unexpected twinkle showed in Jo's eyes for a moment.

"I'll meet her halfway, of course," he said. "And I'll talk to Richard if you think it will help. Does he know about Polly?"

"Most of it," Enid said. "I told him what happened at the auction."

"Well, we'll have to hope he's got enough commonsense to know nonsense when he hears it. Unfortunately he's got no cause to like me."

Richard hadn't, and Enid bit her lip. She and Richard might be lovers now, but it was a new, fragile relationship, and he had loved Gina once, until Jo had taken her away from him. Suppose he believed Gina when she told him — *if* she told him — that Enid and Jo were having an affair, it could completely spoil their happiness, and if he didn't believe Gina it would still strike a very jarring note. Then, suddenly, she thought of Gina . . . *Why* had she been so ready to believe Polly's lies? Was *that* it?

Enid had always thought of Gina as being hard, self sufficient and very self possessed, but perhaps she wasn't as tough as Enid had thought . . .

"Jo," she said impulsively. "Send Gina some flowers — really nice ones, and a letter — she's probably feeling devastated. She's probably sorry, too, now she's had time to think things over. Why not try it?"

"You're a sweet girl, Enid," Jo said huskily. "Maybe I will at that. I'm sorry about all this. Listen, I'd better go now, I should really be in London. I'll give you the number of the hotel

I'll be staying at if anything happens. I should be back tomorrow night."

He dropped a quick unexpected kiss on her forehead and went, leaving Enid a prey to a jumble of conflicting emotions. Even given Polly's wickedly persuasive tongue, Gina's reaction seemed extreme, almost as if she had always been jealous of Enid . . . was that it? Did Gina still love Richard despite everything? Could she just be using Polly's slanderous stories to discredit Enid and Jo and persuade Richard to come back to her?

And if this was so, how would Richard react? Suppose he decided that, after all, it was Gina he wanted? What would happen then? Enid turned icy cold at the thought and the awful thing was, she didn't really know — she didn't know if Richard really loved her or if he regarded their marriage as permanent or not, or if he expected to end it sometime in the future and for them to go their separate ways, as they planned in the original agreement . . .

'I couldn't bear that,' Enid thought. 'I *couldn't*.'

Then, with a sudden lifting of her spirits, she thought 'But he wouldn't be making all these plans to move house if he expected us to split up, he'd stay where he was and wait for a suitable time.'

She got up, mechanically tidying up after their lunch. Jo hadn't eaten much either, he was as upset as she was, and what *was* she going to tell Richard when he got back? Could she possibly get away with telling him nothing? Maybe when Gina cooled down she would realise that there was no truth in what Polly was saying and keep quiet.

'Perhaps I should leave the shop, in spite of what Jo said,' Enid thought. 'I could always tell Richard it was too much of a strain working with Gina's fiancé, he'd accept that.' Or would he? Maybe he would think that Jo had made a real pass at her . . .

But he wouldn't, he's a sweetie, Enid

thought, and opened the shop door for afternoon business. She made a determined effort to forget what had happened, and perhaps fortunately the afternoon was very busy. Customer followed customer in a steady stream, and when she finally locked up she realised that it had been one of the most profitable days for a week.

She walked home slowly, almost expecting Gina to materialise out of some nook or cranny and confront her, but nothing happened, and with a mocking smile at herself she realised that Gina wouldn't start a row in public — she had too much too self respect for that. No, if Gina wanted to start something it would be in private, where she couldn't be overheard, and as she climbed the stairs to the flat Enid found herself glancing apprehensively around, as if Gina was lurking somewhere on the staircase.

"This is silly," she muttered as she let herself into the flat. "She's probably come to her senses by now and she's sorry she made such a fool of herself."

Damn Polly, she thought as she put the kettle on for coffee, why couldn't she keep her mouth shut? The woman was unbalanced, but the trouble was that she was so convincing — she could turn on the charm like a tap, and lie with all the assurance of a confidence trickster . . . perhaps Gina couldn't be blamed too much.

★ ★ ★

Halfway through the evening the phone rang, and with a suddenly dry mouth and a thumping heart Enid picked it up. Even as she drew a deep steadying breath Richard's cheerful voice sounded in her ear, and she closed her eyes in thankfulness. Gina spitting insults on the phone would have been too awful to bear . . .

" . . . wonderful day," Richard was saying happily. "I've nearly got what I wanted already. How are you, darling?"

209

"I'm fine," she lied. There seemed no point in trying to explain the complications of her situation on the phone. "Business is very brisk."

"Great!" Richard exclaimed. "Listen, darling, I must go — there's no phone in my room, I'm on the one in the foyer and someone else wants to use it. I'll be back tomorrow night or the night after. God bless, see you."

There was a click and he was gone. She hung up slowly and sank into a chair, pushing her hair away from her forehead, feeling suddenly exhausted.

'I must go to bed,' she thought. 'I won't be fit for anything in the morning if I don't.'

She lay determinedly reading a book, until the words began to blur, her concentration failed, and she put the light out and fell asleep.

★ ★ ★

She slept better than she had expected to, showered and dressed and forced

210

herself to eat breakfast. Then she walked to work in bright Spring sunshine, and her spirits rose with every step she took. Her fears of the day before seemed faintly ridiculous now, Gina was probably talking to Jo on the phone even now, and if she was still angry there was no way she could get in touch with Richard before Enid had a chance to talk to him first.

Enid unlocked the shop door, tidied up, dusted, and waited for her first customer.

The morning passed uneventfully, but at lunchtime there was a call from Jo. He was speaking from London and he sounded as if he was determined to be cheerful, but she caught the faint undercurrent of strain in his voice.

"Everything OK?" he asked. "No — er — incidents?"

"I haven't walked round and shot Polly, if that's what you mean," Enid forced a smile into her voice. "No, everything's quiet except business, and

211

that's booming. Richard phoned last night but I didn't mention what's happened. Have you heard from — ?"

"From Gina?" A hard edge crept into his voice. "No, I haven't, Enid. Listen, I'll try and look in sometime tomorrow, and Enid — keep cool, won't you? We've done nothing wrong."

"No. Goodbye, Jo."

"Goodbye."

He hung up, and Enid slowly replaced the receiver, biting her lip. It sounded as though Gina was still angry, or perhaps she was hoping to make Jo wriggle a bit longer — she could be playing a dangerous game there though, Jo wasn't the sort of man to be intimidated by that sort of behaviour. Gina could be pushing him too far . . .

Enid went out to lunch though she didn't feel like eating, and deliberately she kept away from the restaurant Jo and she had used. Instead she slipped into a small cafe down a quiet street, fairly confident that if Gina did feel like a confrontation, she wouldn't find Enid in the usual place.

★ ★ ★

Gina didn't appear during the afternoon, and Enid thought she was probably on duty at the hospital. She didn't really expect to see Polly or Mr Hatherley, and Enid shrewdly suspected that he was blissfully unaware of the hornets' nest his wife had stirred up. Perhaps he never would find out, she thought, and perhaps it was better if he didn't.

She locked up and walked home, feeling fractionally less uneasy, but wishing devoutly that Richard would somehow appear and she could tell him what had happened. The trouble was, she still had a niggling, disquieting little doubt that he might take it very badly indeed.

She climbed the stairs, then stopped dead — a girl was standing outside the door, ringing furiously, Enid could hear it from where she stood. Her heart shot

213

into her mouth, then the girl turned her head. It wasn't Gina, it was Penny, Richard's sister.

"Hello," Enid exclaimed, as well as her dry lips would let her. "What are you doing here, Penny? I didn't expect to see you."

"I tried to ring you at the shop but your line was busy whenever I tried." Penny advanced a few steps to meet her, and Enid saw that she was very pale and strained looking. "It — it's Dad, he's had a heart attack. Is Richard anywhere about, Enid?"

"He's in London, doing some research, but he may be home later tonight. Wait, I'll let us in."

She opened the door with fingers that fumbled and shook, and Penny closed it behind them and turned to face her.

"Enid," she said, in tones of quiet despair. "Richard *must* come and see Dad and patch things up with him — I know most of it's Dad's fault, but he really is ill."

"I'm very sorry," Enid said, still shocked. "Is he in hospital?"

"Well, he was until this afternoon, then he discharged himself, would you believe?"

"Yes, I would," Enid said, with more bluntness than tact. "Is he — is he in bed?"

"Yes, and David and I have managed to persuade him to get a private nurse. He grumbled and he's giving her an awful time, but she seems to be able to cope with that. Can we get in touch with Richard, Enid?"

"I'll ring the hotel."

Penny waited while Enid dialled the number, listening to the one-sided conversation intently, and finally Enid hung up and turned to her.

"He's still out, but they're expecting him back later and they'll give him a message. Would you like some coffee, Penny?"

"I'd love a cup," Penny said, smiling faintly. "It's been quite a day."

"Yes, it must have been." Enid went

into the kitchen, and Penny tagged along behind her. "Penny, you do realise that Richard won't — can't — change his mind about his writing?"

"Yes, I understand that," Penny said, perching herself gingerly on the kitchen stool. "But perhaps — " tears came suddenly into her eyes — "perhaps they could — well — make it up?"

"Perhaps," Enid's tone was dry, and Penny shot her a wryly understanding look. "Richard could try, I suppose. But Penny, his father hurt him very badly, you know."

"Yes, I know." Penny blew her nose. "As I said, it's mostly his fault, but Enid, to see him just *lying* there — "

Enid put her arms round her, and Penny cried for a few minutes, then resolutely blew her nose again and straightened her back.

"I'm sorry," she said, firmly. "I didn't mean to fall to pieces like that. It's just that it all happened so quickly, one moment Dad was all right and the next — "

"Heart attacks are like that," Enid said, turning the kettle off. "My father died of one."

"Did he?" Penny looked astonished, then dismayed. "I'm sorry, I didn't know. Was it — quick?"

"Yes, very, almost instantaneous." Enid handed her the coffee mug. "The doctor said he couldn't have known much about it."

"Well, at least Dad's still alive," Penny commented, and Enid thought ruefully:

'Yes, alive, and strong enough to make the nurse's life a misery.'

Then something occurred to her, and she asked:

"Penny, does your father know you've come to see me?"

"No," Penny shook her head, looking guilty. "No, he doesn't."

"He might not be very pleased if Richard turns up uninvited," Enid pointed out. "It could make him worse."

"Yes, I know, but David and I are

prepared to risk that," Penny said, with sudden firmness. "We think they *should* see each other in case — in case — "

'In case the old so and so dies,' Enid thought, but aloud she said:

"I'm sure he won't, Penny — he looked pretty fit to me when I saw him."

"Yes, I heard about that." To Enid's surprise Penny actually smiled. "You stood up to him, didn't you? He rather appreciated that. He said there was more to you than he'd thought and Richard had got a bargain. Enid, would you come and see him?"

"Well, if you think that's all right," Enid said doubtfully. "I might stand up to him again if he was rude about Richard."

"Somehow I don't think that would bother him," Penny said thoughtfully. "I think he took quite a fancy to you."

"I thought he was fond of Gina," Enid said, then bit her lip.

"Well, he was but with reservations," Penny said carefully, after a pause. "I think he thought she was too ambitious."

That word again, Enid thought, but she said nothing, and Penny said:

"Please, Enid, will *you* come? Tomorrow would do."

"Yes, all right, but I can't speak for Richard and I don't know how he'll feel when I tell him," Enid said. "Would the morning do? I can shut the shop for a couple of hours."

"That would be great," Penny exclaimed. "You'd better take a taxi, the bus is a bit unreliable. Unless you'd like me to call for you?"

"A taxi would be fine," Enid said hastily. "Penny, I do hope he's going to be all right."

"So do I," Penny blinked away tears. "I do love him, old so and so that he is. Enid, I *must* go. See you tomorrow."

★ ★ ★

After Penny had left, Enid found she couldn't settle to anything. Had she done the right thing? What would Richard think? Might it be better not to tell him at all? But that was impossible, she had already asked him to phone as a matter of urgency, and in any case he would discover what had happened sooner or later. She prowled round the flat, picking up things and putting them down again, and it was a relief when the phone rang and she heard Richard's voice on the other end.

There was no way in which she could break the news gently, and Richard listened in silence while she explained what had happened.

"I see," he said quietly. "Well, it's up to you if you visit or not — I'll have to think about it, Enid. Don't take any nonsense from him, will you? You don't have to."

"I can cope," Enid said, relieved that he had kept his temper. "When will you be back?"

"Sometime tomorrow, I can't say

exactly when," he replied. "Enid, are you all right? Apart from the news about Dad, I mean?"

For a moment she was tempted to tell him about Gina's quarrel with Jo and her wild accusations, but her courage failed her — it would be difficult enough face to face, but over the phone it seemed impossible, and she had given Richard enough to worry about for one night.

"A bit tired, darling," she said. "We'll talk tomorrow, shall we?"

"Yes, yes of course," Richard said. "Now don't get upset, will you? He's a tough old devil and he'll probably live to be ninety and drive us all potty. Goodnight, darling."

He hung up, and Enid gave a long, tremulous sigh. At least Richard hadn't forbidden her to see his father, he had even said he would think about visiting himself, and that had to be a step in the right direction . . .

She forced herself to eat, then shower and go to bed, and surprisingly she slept quite well. As she ate breakfast, she wondered if she should try to contact Jo to tell him she would be away from the shop for a while, but decided against it. If he rang he would probably assume that she had gone out on business and would ring again.

She phoned for a taxi, then looked at herself critically in the mirror. Pale but well groomed, blue suit immaculate, pale blue blouse clean, shoes shining . . . she would do.

A few minutes later someone knocked on the door, and a man's voice informed her that her taxi had arrived. There was no going back now . . .

★ ★ ★

She chose to sit beside the taxi driver, who was a cheerful middle aged man with a friendly manner, and they chatted quite amiably during the fairly short trip. As they turned into a long curving drive-in flanked by shrubs Enid felt a sudden surge of panic, then hastily suppressed it. She had seen sick people before, Richard's father wouldn't be much different from them ... or would he?

It was Penny who opened the door to the imposing house, almost pulling Enid over the threshold.

"Oh, I'm so glad you've come!" she exclaimed. "He's waiting to see you, I'll take you up."

Enid had just time to notice that there were some beautiful water colours hung on the wall above the curving staircase, and then Penny was pushing a door open, saying:

"Enid's here, Dad — go in, Enid." She stood aside for Enid to enter, said: "I'll be downstairs if you want me, just ring the bell. The nurse has gone outside for a stroll in the garden."

Enid walked slowly into the large bedroom and looked about her. Mr Cummings was lying propped up in bed, but he didn't look pathetic or helpless, far from it. He looked alert, belligerent, and apart from his pallor, reasonably well.

"Come over here," he ordered, and Enid walked to the side of the bed and looked down at him.

"You look better than I thought you would," she said, stifling a suddenly illogical impulse to bend and kiss him. "I thought you'd be strung up to a lot of wires and things."

"I was at first," Mr Cummings said with disgust. "Soon stopped that — made me feel like a defective TV. Well, sit down, girl, I can't talk to you if you hover over me like that."

Enid drew up a chair and sat down, and they eyed each other warily, until he smiled suddenly and she smiled back.

"Thanks for coming," he said, so unexpectedly that Enid's eyes opened wide. "Kind of you."

"That — that's all right," Enid said. "Richard knows, he may come and see you later on, if that's all right."

"Have to be," Mr Cummings said

ungraciously. "Glad you didn't bring me any grapes, I can't stand the things."

Enid, who had thought about that, smiled and said nothing.

"How's that shop of yours going?" he asked. "I thought it looked pretty good when I came in."

"Well, thank you. I didn't think you'd had time to notice," Enid replied drily, and to her surprise he chuckled.

"Spunky little thing, aren't you?" he said. "I like you, Enid."

"Well, thank you," Enid said again. Where *was* this conversation going? She was getting used to his abrupt manner, but what was he trying to do? Enlist her help over Richard, or what?

"It's all right," he said unexpectedly. "I'm not going to try and bribe you because for one thing, I don't think it would work. Enid, you're an intelligent girl, do you think Richard really does have a future as a writer?"

"Yes, I do," she said. "But everything like that takes time, just as I imagine it takes time to build up a business. He's had one novel published as I expect you know, and he's working on another now, but it's not an exact science. I think he'll get there in the end."

"H'm." Mr Cummings grunted. Then he looked keenly at her.

"Fond of him, aren't you?"

Telltale colour washed into her face, and she swallowed hard.

"Thought so," he said, in a satisfied tone. "Good. Gina wasn't, you know, at least I never thought she was — she liked him but that was all. What's this Jo Marsh like?"

"He's a very nice man," Enid said warmly. "Kind but not weak — I like him."

Mr Cummings grunted again, still looking at her.

"Sounds just what Gina needs," he said. "My wife was very fond of Gina but I had my reservations. A bit too fond of money for my liking. Speaking of money, are you two all right?"

"Yes, fine. We — we're doing very well."

"What's this about you selling your flat?" he shot at her, and once again she blinked.

"How did you — oh, I see. Penny."

"Yes, she saw the sign. Wants to make a fresh start somewhere else, does he?"

"That was the idea, yes," she admitted, and Mr Cummings shifted uneasily on his pillows, then fired off another question.

"What about you?" he asked. "You want to move?"

"I — I'll do anything Richard wants," she said, and to her astonishment a large warm hand came out and covered hers, holding it tightly.

"Good girl," he said, then closed his eyes. "Sorry, Enid — feeling a bit tired."

She left her hand where it was until his breathing became soft and regular, then gently withdrew it and went quietly to the bedroom door

and slipped through it. As she went
noiselessly down the stairs she met
Penny waiting anxiously in the hall,
and whispered:

"It's all right, he's asleep. We didn't
have a row. He looks better than I
thought he would."

"Yes, apparently it was only a slight
attack, not as bad as they thought at
first," Penny whispered back. "Oh,
here's nurse — would you like me
to take you to work or will you have
some coffee?"

"Do you mind if we skip the coffee?"
Enid replied. "I really ought to go."

"Right." Penny smiled at the nurse
and led the way to her car. "Thanks
for coming, it couldn't have been easy.
Do you want to check the flat and see
if Richard's back?"

"Yes, that might be a good idea.
Thanks, Penny."

The car started, and Enid glanced
back at the solid prosperous looking
house, wondering at the strange
enigmatic man who was Richard's

father. Autocratic he might be, but there had been real liking and approval in the eyes which had stared at her so intently — was it possible for there to be some sort of family reconciliation? Some sort of compromise? Maybe, maybe not . . . then, as Penny turned the car into the road, Enid knew that she meant to try . . .

9

RICHARD wasn't at home, and Enid wasn't entirely sorry. She needed time to think, and as Penny dropped her outside the shop and drove off, waving goodbye, she stood for a moment on the pavement, collecting her thoughts. It was only eleven o'clock, she hadn't wasted much time, and she unlocked the shop door and went in, stripping off her coat and hanging it up in the back room.

Then, as if someone had waved a wand, the customers began to arrive, and she had a very busy time until at one o'clock she switched the sign to 'Closed' and thankfully locked up.

A sandwich and coffee would do, she decided, and walked round to the small cafe she had used the day before, realising almost with wonder that the sun wasn't just warm, it was

230

hot — Spring really had come at last.

She ate her sandwich and drank her coffee, then walked slowly back to the shop, glancing at her watch to see how much lunch hour she had left. Twenty five minutes, and she meant to take them. Then, as she turned the corner, her heart seemed to catapult into her mouth . . . Gina was there, standing by the door, and even from where Enid was standing her expression was clear — Gina was seething, furiously angry, and there was nothing Enid could do to avoid a confrontation.

Steeling herself, she walked to the shop, unlocked the door and motioned Gina inside, locking it after them.

"You'd better come into the back room," she said quietly. "I'd rather nobody heard our conversation."

Gina walked silently into the privacy of the back of the shop, then turned to face Enid, and despite the fact that she was innocent of any wrongdoing Enid mentally quailed. Gina looked almost murderous; there were huge

231

blue shadows under her eyes, she was white and she even looked thinner.

'She won't listen to a word I say,' Enid thought, and for a moment sheer dismay threatened to overcome her.

"I hope you're pleased with yourself," Gina said, and the venom in her voice couldn't have been bettered, even by Polly Hatherley. "First you steal my fiancé, then you have a disgusting affair with Jo — you're nothing but a slut, Polly had you right the first time she saw you!"

"The first time Polly saw me I was about eight years old," Enid said, her sense of humour choosing the most inopportune moment to erupt. "That's a little young to decide, isn't it?"

"I'm glad you think it's funny," Gina glared. "I don't."

"No, of course it isn't funny." Enid pointed to a chair. "Please, Gina, sit down and try to keep calm — this really isn't helping."

"I'll stand," Gina said stonily. "What have you got to say?"

"Well, first of all let's get one thing straight. I *haven't* been having an affair with Jo, he's a nice guy but I don't feel like that about him and he doesn't feel like that about me. He loves you, Gina, and if you don't believe that then you're a bigger fool than I took you for."

For a moment Gina didn't reply to this blunt statement, then she said:

"Do you really expect me to believe that?"

"Well," Enid gave a little shrug. "I can't make you, of course, but it is the truth and if you don't want to lose Jo you'd better believe it."

Gina said nothing, and Enid went on:

"As for my stealing Richard, I did no such thing. *You* broke off your engagement to be with Jo, I just thought of Richard as my friend. After that happened we decided to team up, and yes, I admit, it was so that Richard could get the money we both felt was rightfully his. Maybe it *wasn't* very ethical, we neither of us felt good about it, but we did it and we've tried to make each other happy. It wasn't the ideal start to a marriage but it seems to be working. I'm sorry Polly came to you making trouble, but she's never liked me, she's absolutely unscrupulous and she can look you in the eye and lie without blinking. I've seen her do it time and again. I've never been anything to her husband but the daughter of a very old friend, whatever she may have said to you, and I've never deliberately made her look stupid in front of a customer or anybody else. Now that's the truth, Gina, take it or leave it."

There was a long pregnant silence, and Enid saw a look of uncertainty cross Gina's face. She bit her lip, shot Enid a questioning look, started to speak, stopped, fumbled in her handbag, fished out a handkerchief, dabbed her eyes with it, and said huskily:

"Are you — are you sure about Jo?

About his loving me?"

"Well, he certainly did at the last count," Enid said, her lips twitching into a smile. "But Gina, he's not the guy to be messed around — if you want him back you'd better do something pretty darned quick."

Gina said nothing, but she turned and walked into the shop, Enid followed her and opened the door. Gina went without a word, and Enid leaned against the wall, her head pounding. That had been frightful, and God only knew what Gina would do now — had she accepted Enid's story? Would she patch things up with Jo? Only time would tell. One thing was absolutely clear, Gina loved Jo, she loved him deeply, more than she had ever loved Richard — if indeed she had ever loved Richard at all. Strange that Richard's father had suspected that . . .

The phone rang and Enid moved to answer it, willing the throbbing in her head to subside, and the voice on the other end of the line was Jo's.

"Are you all right, Enid?" he asked. "I've been trying to get you."

"I'm sorry about that," Enid pulled herself together with a mental jerk. "Richard's father had a heart attack and I went to visit him. It isn't as bad as they thought but he is ill."

"I'm sorry to hear that," Jo exclaimed. "What — will Richard visit, do you think?"

"I'm hoping so," Enid said. "Mr Cummings seems to want some kind of reconciliation."

"Had a good fright, I suppose," Jo said cynically.

"I think it's a bit more than that," Enid said thoughtfully. "It's up to Richard, of course."

"Well, watch it," Jo said. "Ring every coin he gives you."

"Oh, Richard will," Enid said, with a half smile. "Jo, there's something else. Gina came in."

Silence for a moment, then Jo said: "Oh?" in a curiously expressionless voice.

"I told her the truth," Enid said. "I honestly don't know if she accepted it or not, but Jo, she does love you — she loves you very much, she wouldn't have gone over the top like she did otherwise. I think she'll be getting in touch soon. Please, meet her halfway, won't you?"

Another silence, then Jo said:

"Thanks, Enid, I will. Are you going to tell Richard what happened?"

"I think I'd better, in case it gets back to him somehow in some roundabout sort of way, don't you?"

"Courtesy of Polly, for instance?" Jo said. "Yes, perhaps you'd better, Enid, just in case. I'll see you later on this week. Goodbye, and good luck with — with everything."

He hung up, and Enid thought she would certainly need all the luck she could get — she hadn't the remotest idea how Richard would react when she told him about Gina, but instinct urged her to tell anyway. And what about Richard's father?

Someone was trying the shop door, and she went into the shop and opened it, smiling her apologies. It took all her resolution to concentrate on what she was doing, but gradually the turmoil in her emotions began to subside — it looked as though the problem of Gina and Jo was settled, which had to be good — maybe the others would be settled without too much trouble. Or was that too much to hope for?

She half expected Richard to walk in during the afternoon, but he didn't appear, and she wondered if he had gone to the flat, maybe he was waiting to talk to her before he did anything about his father. He could even have tried to phone the shop, but the line had been busy, he might not have been able to get through.

She closed the shop and walked home, and as she climbed the stairs to the flat she saw Richard waiting for her, smiling.

"Hello, darling!" he exclaimed. "How are you?"

"Fine," she lied, as they kissed. "How are you?"

"All right, I guess." He closed the flat door behind them. "I tried to ring but your line was busy. I rang about Dad, he seems to be stable. Stupid old devil, he ought to be in hospital."

"Yes, he ought." Enid smiled. "How long have you been home?"

"I got here about three," Richard said. "Tea, Enid? We'd better have a talk, hadn't we?"

Too right we had, Enid thought as he disappeared into the kitchen, but where do I begin? She sank into an armchair and waited for Richard to come back with the tea, trying to work out how to tell Richard about Gina and Jo, and the more she thought about it the more difficult it seemed to become.

Richard re-appeared with the tea, and she took hers with a murmur of thanks.

"How did you get on with Dad this morning?" he asked, and his tone

239

was too carefully casual — as if he cared and didn't want her to know he did . . .

"Quite well," she said. "Better than I thought I was going to. According to Penny he's taken a fancy to me."

"M'm." Richard grunted. "Well, that shows his good sense, I suppose." He smiled reluctantly. "Tell me exactly what happened."

"I'll try to remember."

She told him quietly and as accurately as she could, and he listened without interrupting. Then he said with the ghost of a smile:

"Strange he should say that about Gina, wasn't it? He's quite observant, but the trouble is . . . "

His voice trailed off as the phone rang, and with a grimace he got up to answer it. Enid put down her cup, listening intently, and it became apparent that it was Penny, and that she was urging Richard to come and visit his father at once.

"Pen, I haven't been home long,

can't it wait till the morning? He's not in immediate danger, is he? No, we're not doing anything else . . . well, all right, but I'm not promising anything."

There was a long pause while Penny either pleaded or ordered, and finally Richard gave his sideways grin and said:

"Oh, all right, we'll come — give us half an hour, will you? And tell the old curmudgeon to keep a civil tongue in his head. Well, he is one, Pen — oh, OK, I won't start anything if he doesn't. See you."

He hung up with a snort and flung out his arms.

"What can you do with her?" he demanded. "She's as obstinate as Dad. She's his natural successor if he'd only admit it. Enid, I'm sorry about this, you've had quite a day, but do you mind going to see him again? It'd keep him quiet for a bit. Perhaps."

"Of course I don't mind." She smiled up at him. "Give me a few minutes to shower and change."

Standing underneath the refreshing flood of water, she thought that at least it put off the evil hour when she told him about Gina, if indeed she could summon up the courage to tell him at all. Suppose he didn't believe her? Suppose he decided the time had come to separate, suppose he wouldn't believe that she really loved him? It was a horrifying thought, and it haunted her during the short drive to his father's house, so that her responses to his strained remarks were even more strained.

Penny and David were there, and judging from the way the front door flew open as soon as they drew up in the drive-in, they had been listening intently for their arrival.

"Hello," Penny said nervously. "How are you?"

"Fine," Richard said curtly. "Upstairs, is he?"

"Yes, the nurse is with him but I think you can go up," David said. "Richard, I know this is hard for you, but if you could — well, be conciliatory, it might help."

Richard nodded without speaking, and Enid saw that a nerve was twitching at the side of his mouth, and knew that his whole body was rigid with tension. She climbed the wide stairs beside him, slipping her hand into his, and he gave it a brief almost perfunctory squeeze.

Mr Cumming's door was slightly open, and Richard paused, then called out:

"Dad, it's us — may we come in?"

The nurse appeared, a pretty dark haired girl with a cheerful calm expression. She greeted them with a tranquil smile.

"Yes, come in, but don't stay too long. I'll be downstairs if you want me."

She left, and they went in.

Richard's father was watching them, his eyes intent, and Enid thought that he looked better than when she had seen him.

"Hello, Enid," he said, then he

243

looked Richard up and down.

"Hello, Richard," he said grimly. "You came, then."

"Of course I came, you're ill," Richard said, sounding exasperated. "How are you, anyway?"

"I'd be better for less fussing," he said. "Sit down."

They complied, and Enid said:

"You look better than you did."

"Slept most of the afternoon," he replied. "New thing for me, that. Didn't like it."

"No, I don't suppose you did, Dad," Richard said. "But if it helps get you better, do it."

"Not much choice with that girl shoving pills into me every five minutes," Mr Cummings said, moving restlessly. "Now then, Richard, about us — you and me. Penny got me your book and I read it."

"And?" Richard asked, as his father paused, for dramatic effect, or so Enid thought.

"It's damned good," Mr Cummings

said, with obvious sincerity. "A damned sight better than I thought it would be. You must get it from your mother. You're talented, just like she was and I think you should go on with it."

There was an electric silence, Richard's jaw dropped, Enid gasped, and Mr Cummings looked at them both and grinned.

"I'm not a complete fool, lad," he said, in a curiously gentle tone. "I admit I'm disappointed — you're my only son but it can't be helped. There it is."

It was Enid who recovered first. She got up, put her arms round him and hugged him, and he hugged her back in a surprisingly strong grip.

"A bit of advice," he said, looking over Enid's bent head at his still speechless son. "You hold on to this girl, she's the one for you, whatever circumstances you married in. Worth three of Gina in my opinion."

"Thanks, Dad, I intend to," Richard said huskily, holding out his hand.

"You — you've got Penny, you know, and David."

Enid raised her tear streaked face, grovelling for a handkerchief.

"Penny's exactly like you, you know," she said. "Daughters often are like their fathers — she'd make a wonderful company director. Girls do all sorts of things these days."

Mr Cummings grunted, but he didn't contradict her. Instead, he gave Richard a sideways look and said:

"Wouldn't take an allowance until you really get going, would you?"

"Certainly not," Richard said firmly. "We'll stand on our own feet, thanks, Dad."

Mr Cummings grunted again.

"About this house move," he said. "Where were you thinking of going?"

"We were going to see a place in Sussex this weekend," Enid told him. "But we could put it off."

"Wouldn't consider somewhere local now we're friends again?" Mr Cummings suggested. "I'd like to see a bit more of you."

"Why not?" Richard smiled. "We'll look around."

"You do that." Suddenly, Mr Cummings looked exhausted. "Let me know how you get on."

With a quick glance at Richard, Enid rose slowly to her feet.

"We'll come and see you again," she said. "And — thank you, Mr Cummings."

"Try 'Dad'," he suggested, and she laughed and kissed him.

She went downstairs before Richard, leaving them both together, and found Penny and David hovering anxiously in the hall.

"It's all right," she whispered. "They've made it up."

"Oh, thank God," Penny exclaimed, and burst into tears.

David pulled her into his arms, smiling shakily at Enid.

"What a relief," he said. "They've both seen sense at last. Come into the lounge and sit down, Enid, you must be exhausted."

He was right, and she sank into a large comfortable armchair with a huge sigh of relief.

"That was really clever of you, giving Dad that book of Richard's," she said to Penny, and Penny's eyes opened wide.

"But — but I didn't," she said, and then laughed.

"He bought it himself," she said. "But he wasn't going to admit it, not yet, anyway."

David grinned and Enid laughed, and Richard appeared, pale but smiling.

"He's tired and he wants to go to sleep," he said. "He wants the nurse to come and shove whatever he's got to swallow into him now and be done with it."

"That poor girl," Penny said, but she smiled. "Will you stay for dinner, you two?"

"Thanks, but we've got some things to discuss," Richard said quietly. "We'll be in touch as soon as we can."

They said goodbye and got into the car, and Enid leaned back with a deep, relieved sigh.

"That's that, then," she said. "Richard, I'm so glad — I *hated* you being at loggerheads with your father."

"I didn't enjoy it myself," he admitted. "And neither did Dad though he wouldn't admit it. Enid," he hesitated momentarily "would you mind if we stayed here, in the district, I mean? Or would you rather get away, make a fresh start?"

"That's a tempting thought," she said. "If we stay around here we'll run into Gina from time to time, and there's Jo — Richard, there's something I *must* tell you."

He shot her a half alarmed, half questioning look, then said quietly:

"Can it wait till we get home? There's something I have to tell you, too."

Apprehension gripped her suddenly — what was he going to say? Surely, not that he wanted to end their marriage? Not now, when things were going so well . . . she studied his expression surreptitiously, but his face gave nothing away, and she sat in silence until they reached the flat and he stopped the car.

"I'll put the car away, shan't be a minute," he said. "Got your key?"

She nodded dumbly, got out, and went slowly up the stairs, her apprehension turning to near panic. Her fingers felt stiff as she fumbled with the door key, switched on the light, and went over to the window to draw the curtains. Dusk was falling and a bat swooped across the house roofs, startling her. What was it doing flying over a town? Was it as lost as she felt?

Richard had told his father he intended to hold on to her, but suppose he had said that to please him? It was possible — people did that to placate sick people, then did what they really wanted to do when that person recovered — was Richard doing that?

Then she heard him push open the door and come in, and turned.

"Right, then," he said, smiling, but the twitching muscle at the corner of his mouth was back. "Confession time, or whatever — you go first, darling."

"Shall we sit down?" she suggested, huskily, and he seated himself opposite her, his eyes on her face.

"It — it might take a little while," she said. "It's about Gina — Gina and Jo, really. Polly got at Gina and somehow convinced her that Jo and I were having an affair, which we weren't. She accused Jo, they had a tremendous row, Jo told me, then Gina came round to the shop to have it out with me."

She paused, and Richard said quietly: "Go on."

"We had a pretty heavy scene," Enid said, trying to smile. "I think I managed to persuade her to see the truth, but one thing's certain, Richard. She loves Jo, she really loves him, and I hope that by now they've made it up."

"How do you feel about Jo?" Richard asked, still quietly.

"I like him very much, he's a nice guy," Enid said sincerely. "But I don't feel anything else for him — I don't think I ever would — you see, I love you."

Richard stared at her, then leaned forward in his chair, seized her hands, and gripped them so tightly that she almost cried out.

"Say that again," he whispered. "That last bit."

"I love you," she whispered back, and tears began to pour down her face. "I *love you*, Richard."

"Oh, Enid, darling," he said, in a strange hoarse voice. "I love you, too."

"W-what?"

"I love you." He took her wet face between his hands. "I love you, I have loved you for weeks now — long before we actually *made* love. I've been so scared you'd want out if I told you — I wanted to a dozen times, but I

252

wasn't sure how you felt about me. Are you absolutely *sure*, Enid?"

"I've never been so sure about anything," Enid said, reaching up and catching his hands. "I was scared to tell you, too — I thought you might still be in love with Gina."

"And I was scared you might fall for that bastard Jo," Richard said. "Only, he's not a bastard, is he? What happened to him and Gina could happen to anyone — she was right to break our engagement, I know that now. I'm thankful she did or we'd never have got together, would we?"

"No, I don't suppose we would." Enid slipped her arms round his neck and he drew her into his arms, almost as if she was a fragile, delicate thing. "Richard, I'm so happy."

"So am I," he said. "We've been a couple of fools, haven't we?"

"I guess so." She snuggled close into his embrace, feeling his heart beating under her damp cheek. "We can have a proper marriage now, can't we?"

"Oh yes." He kissed her, slowly and lingeringly, then, suddenly, he chuckled. "And I'd better hold on to you, or Dad will kill me."

"If I don't kill you first," she smiled in her turn. "Richard, I couldn't bear to lose you."

"Or I you." He looked down at her, his smile unsteady, tears in his eyes. "Enid, we must talk — about our future, about everything."

"Yes." She put up her hand and ran it gently along his cheek. "Yes, there's a lot to discuss."

They sat in silence, pressed closely together, savouring the overwhelming feeling of happiness that engulfed them, and Enid thought 'This is the real beginning — the beginning of a real, proper marriage. We can be open and honest with each other from now on — open and honest and *loving* . . . '

Other titles in the Linford Romance Library:

A YOUNG MAN'S FANCY
Nancy Bell

Six people get together for reasons of their own, and the result is one of misunderstanding, suspicion and mounting tension.

THE WISDOM OF LOVE
Janey Blair

Barbie meets Louis and receives flattering proposals, but her reawakened affection for Jonah develops into an overwhelming passion.

MIRAGE IN THE MOONLIGHT
Mandy Brown

En route to an island to be secretary to a multi-millionaire, Heather's stubborn loyalty to her former flatmate plunges her into a grim hazard.

WITH SOMEBODY ELSE
Theresa Charles

Rosamond sets off for Cornwall with Hugo to meet his family, blissfully unaware of the shocks in store for her.

A SUMMER FOR STRANGERS
Claire Hamilton

Because she had lost her job, her flat and she had no money, Tabitha agreed to pose as Adam's future wife although she believed the scheme to be deceitful and cruel.

VILLA OF SINGING WATER
Angela Petron

The disquieting incidents that occurred at the Vatican and the Colosseum did not trouble Jan at first, but then they became increasingly unpleasant and alarming.

DOCTOR NAPIER'S NURSE
Pauline Ash

When cousins Midge and Derry are entered as probationer nurses on the same day but at different hospitals they agree to exchange identities.

A GIRL LIKE JULIE
Louise Ellis

Caroline absolutely adored Hugh Barrington, but then Julie Crane came into their lives. Julie was the kind of girl who attracts men without even trying.

COUNTRY DOCTOR
Paula Lindsay

When Evan Richmond bought a practice in a remote country village he did not realise that a casual encounter would lead to the loss of his heart.

ENCORE
Helga Moray

Craig and Janet realise that their true happiness lies with each other, but it is only under traumatic circumstances that they can be reunited.

NICOLETTE
Ivy Preston

When Grant Alston came back into her life, Nicolette was faced with a dilemma. Should she follow the path of duty or the path of love?

THE GOLDEN PUMA
Margaret Way

Catherine's time was spent looking after her father's Queensland farm. But what life was there without David, who wasn't interested in her?

HOSPITAL BY THE LAKE
Anne Durham

Nurse Marguerite Ingleby was always ready to become personally involved with her patients, to the despair of Brian Field, the Senior Surgical Registrar, who loved her.

VALLEY OF CONFLICT
David Farrell

Isolated in a hostel in the French Alps, Ann Russell sees her fiancé being seduced by a young girl. Then comes the avalanche that imperils their lives.

NURSE'S CHOICE
Peggy Gaddis

A proposal of marriage from the incredibly handsome and wealthy Reagan was enough to upset any girl — and Brooke Martin was no exception.

A DANGEROUS MAN
Anne Goring

Photographer Polly Burton was on safari in Mombasa when she met enigmatic Leon Hammond. But unpredictability was the name of the game where Leon was concerned.

PRECIOUS INHERITANCE
Joan Moules

Karen's new life working for an authoress took her from Sussex to a foreign airstrip and a kidnapping; to a real life adventure as gripping as any in the books she typed.

VISION OF LOVE
Grace Richmond

When Kathy takes over the rundown country kennels she finds Alec Stinton, a local vet, very helpful. But their friendship arouses bitter jealousy and a tragedy seems inevitable.

CRUSADING NURSE
Jane Converse

It was handsome Dr. Corbett who opened Nurse Susan Leighton's eyes and who set her off on a lonely crusade against some powerful enemies and a shattering struggle against the man she loved.

WILD ENCHANTMENT
Christina Green

Rowan's agreeable new boss had a dream of creating a famous perfume using her precious Silverstar, but Rowan's plans were very different.

DESERT ROMANCE
Irene Ord

Sally agrees to take her sister Pam's place as La Chartreuse the dancer, but she finds out there is more to it than dyeing her hair red and looking like her sister.

HEART OF ICE
Marie Sidney

How was January to know that not only would the warmth of the Swiss people thaw out her frozen heart, but that she too would play her part in helping someone to live again?

LUCKY IN LOVE
Margaret Wood

Companion-secretary to wealthy gambler Laura Duxford, who lived in Monaco, seemed to Melanie a fabulous job. Especially as Melanie had already lost her heart to Laura's son, Julian.

NURSE TO PRINCESS JASMINE
Lilian Woodward

Nick's surgeon brother, Tom, performs an operation on an Arabian princess, and she invites Tom, Nick and his fiancé to Omander, where a web of deceit and intrigue closes about them.

THE WAYWARD HEART
Eileen Barry

Disaster-prone Katherine's nickname was "Kate Calamity", but her boss went too far with an outrageous proposal, which because of her latest disaster, she could not refuse.

FOUR WEEKS IN WINTER
Jane Donnelly

Tessa wasn't looking forward to meeting Paul Mellor again — she had made a fool of herself over him once before. But was Orme Jared's solution to her problem likely to be the right one?

SURGERY BY THE SEA
Sheila Douglas

Medical student Meg hadn't really wanted to go and work with a G.P. on the Welsh coast although the job had its compensations. But Owen Roberts was certainly not one of them!

HEAVEN IS HIGH
Anne Hampson

The new heir to the Manor of Marbeck had been found. But it was rather unfortunate that when he arrived unexpectedly he found an uninvited guest, complete with stetson and high boots.

LOVE WILL COME
Sarah Devon

June Baker's boss was not really her idea of her ideal man, but when she went from third typist to boss's secretary overnight she began to change her mind.

ESCAPE TO ROMANCE
Kay Winchester

Oliver and Jean first met on Swale Island. They were both trying to begin their lives afresh, but neither had bargained for complications from the past.

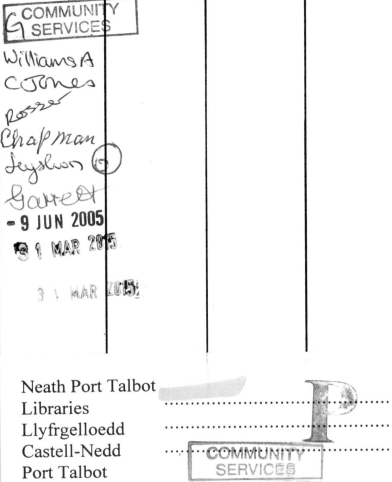